Praise for
Grand Prix de Littérature Policière nominee
Benjamin Whitmer
and *Cry Father*

"Whitmer peels back the layers to reveal a masculine world of no limits and no rules. With each wild turn of events, this novel continues to intrigue."

—*Library Journal*

"*Cry Father* is strong medicine. It burns going down, but there's healing in that dose as well. It's a book that put me in the mind of my own Dad and made me think of my own duties as a father. And any book that can reach inside your heart and mind and force you to reflect on such things is doing something very, very right indeed."

—Craig Davidson, author of *Rust and Bone*
and *Cataract City*

"I've been carrying *Cry Father* around since I finished it, opening it randomly and reading a paragraph or two when I'm otherwise idly waiting. . . . No, it isn't that good; it's much, much better. . . . It will shock you, astound you, make you laugh and break your heart. . . . Just try to stop reading."

—*Bookreporter*

"A gut-punch of raw storytelling power. A novel of fathers and sons, and the constant—and at times emotionally crippling—mistakes both make. Much like Whitmer's first novel, it is absolutely uncompromising and one of the year's must-read novels."

—*LitReactor*

"Whitmer writes about the rustbelt of life. Showing the seedy, the dark, and the things that others are afraid to show."

—Frank Bill, author of *Crimes in Southern Indiana*

"The bleak world of *Cry Father* is filled with the guns, booze, cigarettes, and pick-ups fans of rural noir have come to love but such elements never approach cliché in their handling. Whitmer is trying to say something about loss and fathers and sons yet offers no answers, just human truths and timeless questions. The novel reads faster than the most structurally precise thrillers."

—*Spinetingler Magazine*

"Whitmer's bleak tale of dysfunctional father-son relationships contains some shockingly violent scenes, captures the seedy milieus of rundown mountain towns, and tallies the enormous cost of loving and losing."

—*Booklist*

"Gritty and gruesome. . . . With an explosive finale . . . this bloodbath isn't for the faint of heart or stomach."

—*Publishers Weekly*

"A first-rate addition to the canon of 'rural noir' storytelling. . . . An accomplished, swaggering tale of battered-but-still-striving men living in the no-man's-land of southeast Colorado. . . . Whitmer is one helluva storyteller, and *Cry Father* nails it on all fronts."

—Shelf Awareness

"A grim piece of storytelling . . . but thanks to Whitmer's conversational, darkly humorous prose, the reader never really feels weighed down. . . . *Cry Father* is by no means a traditional crime novel. In fact, I would be hard-pressed to even call it one. Or maybe it's simply the evolution of the crime novel, where there are no clearly defined roles, no paint-by-the-number heroes and villains, no one to cheer for or to revile. If that's the case, I welcome it with open arms."

—Los Angeles Review of Books

"The writing combines the best elements of noir with emotional grittiness and a degree of physical violence that wouldn't be out of place in a horror book, but the author brings them together with such unpretentious elegance that the end result can only be described as beautiful. . . . Whitmer is a superb observer with a knack for detail and metaphor."

—Bookslut

"Searing, spare, beautiful prose and characters who arrive on the page already well-worn. A pebble tossed into this novel reveals concentric waves of violence, guilt, culpability, shame, and vengeance—and yet when the surface settles, astonishingly, there is hope."

—Sophie Littlefield, author of *Garden of Stones*
and *The Missing Place*

Cry Father

BENJAMIN WHITMER

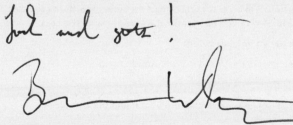

G

GALLERY BOOKS

NEW YORK   LONDON   TORONTO   SYDNEY   NEW DELHI

G

Gallery Books
An Imprint of Simon & Schuster, Inc.
1230 Avenue of the Americas
New York, NY 10020

First Gallery Books trade paperback edition May 2015

GALLERY BOOKS and colophon are registered trademarks of Simon & Schuster, Inc.

For information about special discounts for bulk purchases, please contact Simon & Schuster Special Sales at 1-866-506-1949 or business@simonandschuster.com.

The Simon & Schuster Speakers Bureau can bring authors to your live event. For more information or to book an event contact the Simon & Schuster Speakers Bureau at 1-866-248-3049 or visit our website at www.simonspeakers.com.

Interior design by Jaime Putorti

Manufactured in the United States of America

10 9 8 7 6 5 4 3 2 1

Library of Congress Cataloging-in-Publication Data is available.

ISBN 978-1-4767-3436-1 (pbk)
ISBN 978-1-4767-3437-8 (ebook)

For Max Moody and Grace Roselee,

who had one of the best fathers I ever knew.

Therefore I say to son or daughter who has no pleasure in the name Father, "You must interpret the word by all that you have missed in life. Every time a man might have been to you a refuge from the wind, a covert from the tempest, the shadow of a great rock in a weary land, that was a time when a father might have been a father indeed."

—George MacDonald

bottles

Patterson Wells walks through the front door to find Chase working on a heap of crystal meth the size of his shrunken head.

"Sit down, motherfucker," Chase says, perched birdlike on the couch, his eyes smoking like he's been shooting the shit straight into his tear ducts. Patterson eases down into the only other seat in the room, a white leather recliner that leans to the side like a heap of dirty laundry, while Chase chops a line of meth and waves at Patterson to fall to.

It's only been two weeks since Patterson saw him last, but Chase has lost a good twenty pounds, and Patterson's pretty sure he's wearing the same soiled tank top that he'd been wearing when he rolled off the job site. "You got anything else?" he asks.

"Like what?" Chase asks.

Patterson rubs his eyes. It's been a very long drive. "I wouldn't say no to a beer."

"I got pop if you want some." There's plastic bottles staggered all over the coffee table. At least one of them gone bulbous, some liquid that doesn't look at all like pop leaking from under the cap. "You better let me check them first though," he continues. "Some of them's full of piss."

"I'm all right," Patterson says.

"Bet it smells like piss in here, too." Chase sniffs the air. "Does it stink?"

Patterson nods, looking at the bottles. His eyes are watering at the smell. Then he shakes his head. "We still going fishing?" he asks.

Chase lights a cigarette and tosses the match into a heavy glass ashtray on the coffee table already overflowing with butts. He clutches up, giggling, smoke erupting out of his mouth and nose. "My fucking skin itches," he sputters, scratching red welts down his arms.

"Well." Patterson slaps his knees and stands.

"Hold on." Chase stops laughing abruptly. "You ain't got to leave. I got something else." He pulls a fifth of Evan Williams out of the couch cushions, tosses it to Patterson. "I keep it around for when I'm coming off the shoulder." He rattles out another laugh. "But mostly I'd rather get high again."

Patterson takes a drink of the bourbon and sits back down. "When'd you start dealing meth?"

Chase's eyes bulge in his head. The left eye more than the right. "You a fucking cop?"

"No, I ain't a fucking cop," Patterson says. "But I saw you two weeks ago and you didn't have no meth empire."

"My bitch set this up," Chase says. "Goddamn, that itches. I come home and found my kitchen turned into a meth lab, her fucking some biker motherfucker on the floor. He's out in the backyard."

Patterson tightens the cap down on the bottle of whiskey.

"Shut the fuck up." Chase lets out a machine gun burst of laughter, his cheekbones punching through his yellow skin. "You really think I stabbed some motherfucker in the neck and then buried him in the backyard? And then told you about it? Shut the fuck up."

Patterson stands. "Bathroom?"

Chase jerks his head at a hallway by the entrance to the kitchen. "First door."

Patterson pisses into the toilet. Leaning against the wall, his vision swimming. He's so tired the back of his neck aches and his knees feel loose. He finishes pissing, pulls off his battered Avrilla ball cap, and runs water to wash his face. He looks worn-out in the mirror, he looks spent, he looks like he's not too far off a meth bender himself. And the idea of maybe doing a line or two just to wake up does flash through his mind. Then he hears it. It sounds like breathing. And whatever it is, it's coming from right behind him, from the tub.

Patterson puts his hand on the .45 he carries in an inside-the-waistband holster just behind his right hip, then shuts the water off.

It's breathing, all right. And it's coming harder. Thrashing. Grunting, snorting, like there's some kind of miniature pig running back and forth, ramming its head into the sides of the tub.

Patterson slides the back of his hand onto the edge of the shower curtain. He tightens his fingers around the grip of his gun and pushes the curtain back just far enough to peek into the tub.

She's naked, hogtied with thin nylon cord, a strip of black duct tape across her mouth. Her blue eyes pleading at Patterson, black mascara streaking down her face.

Patterson's legs wobble, threaten to give altogether. He forces himself to kneel and pulls the duct tape free of her mouth. "Are you all right?"

She croaks something.

Patterson flips open his clip knife, cuts her hands free. Then leans across her bare body, white and flat and lined with blue veins, and cuts the rope around her feet. She sobs, stifles it. Patterson pulls a towel off the rack, wraps it around her shoulders. "I'll be right back," he says. "You stay here."

She nods, rubbing her wrists.

Patterson rises, drawing his .45. Exhausted. He walks back out into the living room and stands by the hallway, holding the gun behind his right leg.

"Did you see my bitch in there?" Chase has the remote control, flipping channels on a little television set on a stand against the wall. "Her name's Mel. Mel, Patterson. Patterson, Mel. That's why I been pissing in these bottles. Every time I go in there she goes ape shit. And I can't piss with somebody watching, especially if they're making a bunch of noise."

"She been in there since you found her with the biker?" Patterson asks.

Chase's hand shoots into the pillows of the couch and stays there. Patterson's elbow twitches, but he doesn't raise the .45. "What the fuck do you know about the biker?" Chase says. His eyes are bulging again, threatening to bust like the pop bottles on the table.

"Easy," Patterson says. "I only know what you told me."

Chase draws his hand out from the couch, empty. "You want to fuck her?"

Patterson shakes his head. "Not even a little," he says.

"Fifty dollars. You don't even have to untie her."

"I don't want to fuck her."

"Twenty dollars."

Patterson doesn't bother answering.

The volume on the television is muted, the shows flickering past. Sports, news, cartoons. It's been a long time since Patterson has seen a television. "If you'd have said yes, I'd have shot you," Chase says.

"I know it," Patterson says. He steps back, putting some space between him and Chase. Then he brings his .45 up. "Don't reach in the couch."

Chase looks at him. "What the fuck are you doing?"

"I can't leave her like that."

"You can't leave her like that. You don't know that cunt. Fuck you, you can't leave her."

"Come on," Patterson says.

"Come on where?"

"Wherever you keep the rope," Patterson says. "It's your turn."

Chase stands. "You ain't going to make it out of here, you brave motherfucker." He licks his lips. "I'm going to cut that bitch's throat and you're going to watch. That's what I'm going to do." He struts into the hallway. "You're a cunt, too."

She rams him straight in the face with the barrel of a baseball bat. Chase stumbles back, blood flushing from his flattened nose. She'd been standing around the corner, just far enough back in the hallway that they couldn't see her. Chase swats at her, his eyelids fluttering. She swings from her shoulders, the barrel of the bat thudding into the side of his skull. He falls prone, his eyeballs flickering back and forth behind his lids.

She stands over him, the baseball bat cocked. Still naked. Hairless and small-breasted, her skin loose on her frame like badly fit clothes. Chase's left knee twitches. Then twitches again. Then starts to shake. She spits in his face and stalks back down the hall.

Patterson holsters his .45 and manages to get a cigarette out of his pack. And using both hands to steady the flame, to get it lit. Chase's leg is still going, blood running out of his nose and ears, pooling under his head. Patterson smokes the cigarette, wishing more than a little that the leg would stop shaking.

She returns dressed in a pair of jeans and a Steve Earle T-shirt, her face scrubbed clean, her skin unhealthily translucent without makeup. She's carrying a duffel bag.

"You need a ride anywhere?" Patterson asks.

"Where'd you get the cigarette?"

Patterson passes her one. She lights it and her eyes blank with pleasure. "Jesus, I needed that."

"How long were you in there?" Patterson asks.

"A day. Maybe." She steps forward and kicks Chase in the side, hard. Breath whistles out of him. "He'll be fine."

"Is there a dead biker in the backyard?" Patterson asks.

She snorts. "He got that off some dipshit TV show. He's been up six fucking days."

"Right," Patterson says. "No ride?"

She shakes her head. "I'll take his car. The motherfucker."

Patterson closes the door behind him, quietly. Leaving her to it.

Justin

I can't pretend it ain't hard to get back to writing to you. I don't do
it at all when I'm on the job. When I'm climbing trees twelve hours
a day, I don't have to worry about the proper handling of my own
memories. By the second day on a job, I'm too tired to put pen to
paper anyway. And even if I could stay awake to write, I can't imagine
a better way to piss off a work crew than to keep a light on so's I could
put my feelings down in some notebook. I'd be lucky not to find my
harness cut the next day. The men I work with, they don't grieve.
They drink, then they erupt.

This year's work season was the roughest I've had in a while.
There was a tropical storm that hit Texas in August and it took out
most of the power in the southern half of the state. They were offering double time clearing power lines, which I couldn't pass up, but it
was the worst kind of work. Eighteen-hour days, with six hours off to
try to get a little sleep in the tent city they'd set up for us, no hot meals

but what we could cook on campfires. But I figured since I started early maybe I'd knock off in March. Not that it worked out that way, of course. It never does. I ended up in Missouri, South Dakota, Virginia, and then, after a freak spring storm, down in Florida. Which is why it's now May and I'm just getting free.

I'm not ready to drive back to the mesa yet, I'll tell you that. I need some space before making that particular drive. Some years it takes me weeks to make it back home. Driving in thousand-mile loops, sleeping in campgrounds, figuring out what to do with myself when I don't have work to keep my mind off you. This year I was supposed to have two weeks of camping in the Ozarks with a buddy of mine but it fell through in a big way. In fact, I'm writing this in the cab of my truck in East St. Louis, about a mile from his house. I'm worn so thin you could put your finger right through me like tissue.

The thing is, it's the driving that's probably the worst of it. Knowing that I should be coming home to you. Knowing that I'm not. I don't know how your mother does it, still living in the same house where you died, still eating at the same kitchen table where we used to feed you. I can't even listen to the same music I listened to back then. Chase made fun of me all season, finding old country music cassettes in the truck. I didn't tell him that I wasn't listening to it because I liked it much, just that it was the only thing I wasn't listening to at any point when you were alive.

That's what the drive is like. It's like every song you and I used to listen to together playing at once. All the ones I used to sing to you at bedtime. The old gut-sick pain has died out, and I don't have to pull off by the side of the road shaking too hard to drive anymore, but it's still like somebody's peeled off the top couple layers of my skin. I don't even bother trying to stop for sleep or food. I just white-knuckle it the whole way.

maps

Patterson sits in the parking lot of a cinder-block bar at the bottom of the I-70 ramp. Lit by the dome light of his Ford Ranger, staring at the ruled schoolboy notebook he writes to his son in. Then, nothing left to write, he puts the notebook in his Alice pack and pulls out a road atlas. East St. Louis. East St. Louis to where? There has to be somewhere else besides the mesa. Montana, maybe. Or the Black Hills. There's nothing like the Black Hills in spring. It'd be chilly at night this time of year, but daytime'd be perfect. He and Sancho could live out of the tent for a couple of weeks. The dog could run around and chase all the animals he wanted.

But maps never do him any good, not when he's already set on the mesa. So he folds the atlas closed and stares at the I-70 ramp. Then at the cinder-block bar, thinking about going inside and getting good and drunk. But he knows better than that, too. Knows that drunk's just about the last thing he needs to be. The bar looks like it's undergone a disaster of its own, the cinder block pitted and blasted and the steel door slightly crumpled, as though it's been ruffled by a minor hurricane. Patterson's always surprised at how far gone everything is when he comes out of the rubble at the end of a season. The thing about working in disaster areas is that you expect that the rest of the country is doing better. And it could be that there are parts that are. Somewhere along the coasts, maybe, where the people who matter live. But the interior is perpetually rolling wreckage, and the ruin visited by hurricane isn't even different in degree from the ruin found in your average midwestern city.

That shows in the bars like nowhere else. The bars are identical. You'd be surprised, but no matter how bad it is, there are always bars. Somebody was serving drinks in New Orleans the day after the levees broke, that's a guarantee. All the hospitals were flooded, the churches closed, but there was some joint serving straight whiskey to disaster-addled drunks the next day, even if it was over a plywood and sawhorse counter. And those ad hoc bars you'll find in disaster areas, they're no more disheartening than your average rust-belt beer joint.

Which is why Patterson really doesn't want to get up and go inside this one. But he can't remember the last time he ate, and he knows that once he starts the drive for real, there's no stopping for anything but gas. Besides, he's twitching for a drink. Not a dozen, he tells himself, but one very stiff one. Maybe two. So he reaches behind his seat, scratches Sancho on the head, not even eliciting a whine from the sleeping dog, and opens the door of his truck.

It's just as bad as he expected inside.

"What can I get you?" the bartender asks.

Patterson takes a stool, dumping his Alice pack on the floor next to him. "You serve food?"

The bartender nods at a snack machine by the door. Pork rinds and miniature donuts. "Got frozen pizzas in the back, too. But you're going to have to order a drink."

"Give me a beer. And a shot of Beam. A double."

The bartender pours the bourbon and hands it to Patterson, the beer following. Patterson drinks the bourbon straight off.

It's just then that he hears the door open behind him. And the rust-belt warriors who occupy the shadows of the bar all turn in a pack. Eyeballing what comes through the door with the kind of interest that wild dogs reserve for fresh meat. She sits down next to Patterson, wearing a hooded sweatshirt over her Steve Earle shirt and a pair of engineer boots that add an inch to her height. "Looking for food," Mel says to the bartender.

The bartender sighs as if this line of inquiry is a calamity that just won't end. His head makes the slightest movement toward the snack machine.

"They have frozen pizzas in back, too," Patterson offers. "But you have to order a drink."

"Good." She drops a fresh pack of Marlboros and a new Bic lighter on the bar. "Beer?"

"Bud Select?" the bartender says.

She peels the cellophane from her cigarettes. "Why Bud Select?"

"A lot of the women who come in here like it."

"That's fine," she says.

"It's just one, really," he says.

She lights her cigarette and blows smoke at him.

"The woman who comes in here. She lives next door and she's almost blind. It's the only place that serves alcohol that she can find."

"Bud Select is fine," she repeats.

The bartender pulls the tap handle and watches her. "Where you headed?"

"Just passing through."

"I think I've seen you before." He passes her the glass.

"You haven't. What about the pizza?"

The bartender lifts his hands in surrender and moves down the bar toward the flap, heading for the back.

Mel rests her cigarette in an ashtray and blows her red nose in one of the cocktail napkins, then folds it in half and blows her nose again.

"I can drive you." It's a big man in a flannel shirt. A port-wine stain running from his forehead down into his bushy beard.

She crumples up the napkin and drops it in the ashtray, taking up her cigarette again.

"You're walking, right?" He winks down the bar at a little man in the shadows. "I didn't hear no car before you came in."

"Easy," Patterson says, without looking at him.

"Easy yourself, motherfucker," he returns. "I was talking to the lady. Offering her a ride."

She looks tired. Very tired. But not even a little scared. "If I decide to take you up on it, I'll let you know," she says.

"Whatever you say," the man says. "Just trying to be friendly."

Patterson lifts his Alice pack and takes out his road atlas again. Hoping there's some magic route that he's going to land on just by opening it. But knowing that once it's time to start the trip back to the mesa, there's no stopping it, that it's like a runaway train rolling under its own inertia. And also knowing that he's mostly trying to ignore Mel sitting there.

"You either got it all figured out or you're starting all the way over," Mel says, her voice close at hand. Her face leans in on his as she checks out the atlas, open to Colorado.

"I had it all figured out," Patterson says.

She leans back from him. "And now?"

"And now the San Luis Valley." Patterson closes the atlas. "Did Chase wake up?"

"Fuck Chase." She lets the final hit from her cigarette float out of her mouth on a sigh. Then she lights a second cigarette with a kind of reckless gusto, only letting off the lighter after scorching it halfway to the filter. "Fuck Chase."

"I'll drink to that," Patterson says, and does.

"You some kind of one percenter?" she asks.

"One percenter?"

"The tattoos."

"I'm a tree trimmer," Patterson says. "That's how I know Chase. Worked with him. We were supposed to go fishing."

"A tree trimmer." She runs her fingers over his forearm, purple with ink. Patterson catches a glimpse of Port-Wine Stain, who looks likely to start gnawing chunks out of his beer glass. "So where'd you get them all?"

"That's a long story," Patterson says. "Most of them are cover-ups."

Even her grin is crooked. "I know some guys covering up the same, I think." She stands. "Would you do me a favor?"

"Probably."

"I need to use the bathroom. Would you watch my cigarettes?"

"That I can do."

When she's gone, Port-Wine Stain lifts his beer at Patterson. "Looks like you got her all figured out."

"I ain't got anything figured out," Patterson says.

"Sure you do." His ruined face carries all the pride and guts that comes with living in a town full of crumbling factories. "This ain't your bar, buddy. This ain't even your fucking town." He fumbles his shirt up, his hand shaking with alcoholic palsy. A snub-nose .38, shelved in a white roll of fat.

"Settle down, Vince," the bartender says to him. "You ain't shooting anyone in here."

The man lets his shirt fall over his gun. "I can wait until he walks out."

When Mel returns from the bathroom, Patterson slings his Alice pack over his shoulder and stands.

"We ain't got our pizza," Mel protests.

"I don't recommend waiting on it."

"Suit yourself," she says, sitting. "Make sure you don't get too far down the road before you turn around."

"I suggest you walk out with me," Patterson says.

"I ain't leaving without my pizza," she says.

As Patterson pushes through the door, Port-Wine Stain laughs a rolling whiskey laugh that makes the point between his shoulder blades twitch. But you can't tell anybody anything, and he can't imagine anything good coming out of any time spent in the woman's company.

implosion

The first three-quarters of the drive is interstate. It's semis and vaca-tioners, truck stops for coffee and cigarettes, whatever country music station flashes across the plains until it doesn't anymore. The sun ris-ing and traveling across the wide-open Missouri sky and then falling in Kansas and nowhere to be seen again in Colorado.

It's a heavy drive, almost like falling. A drive like toward some planetary mass, with the broken plateau around Walsenburg, Colo-rado, being the bottom. And then it's up again, through the La Veta Pass, where the sky lowers to ten feet off the ground and the tempera-ture plummets by double digits. And Patterson's up through the pass, and in an instant the clouds are gone and the sky is a sudden blue, and he's looping through the Sangre de Cristos in easy arcs, through moun-tainsides dressed in lodgepole pine and the last rags of spring snow.

By the time he clears the pass into the San Luis Valley, entering the A-frames and manufactured homes of Fort Garland, Colorado, population four hundred, Patterson's almost excited to get to the cabin. He hasn't slept in nearly two days, but he's not tired, not even a little bit, spinning the truck south onto CO-159, aiming at a massive gray storm front ten miles down the road.

And he does the first thing he always does when he makes the San Luis Valley. He spins the radio dial until he finds Brother Joe's voice. Brother Joe's ranting about the group of international bankers who blew up the World Trade Center on September 11, 2001, and then blamed it on the Arabs. About the Israelis who got the warning and escaped. About implosion patterns.

Patterson drifts somewhere between his cigarette smoke and Brother Joe's tinny voice. The radio man sounds like home. A patch of fresh rain, wet highway, then the storm. Heavy drops of rain bullet the windshield and Sancho wakes, making a pantherlike growl in the back of his throat. Patterson reaches around to stroke his shivering neck, and the dog whines for a minute or two, then falls asleep again as they exit the storm into a grayish spatter of sunlight and the village of San Luis.

It's one gas station and three bars, all of which open sometime after four and close at eleven, the Sangre de Cristo church overlooking the town to make sure of it. Patterson parks on the main drag and cruises the short aisles of the R&R Market, pulling water, bacon, and canned goods into his cart. The woman behind the counter watches him with the same amount of interest she has for the insects let in by the warped screen door.

horses

The truck's tires skew in the dirt as they switchback up the mesa onto a plateau of blue-gray rabbit brush and sage, skirting the small ponds left in the road from the short storm. Then Patterson has to brake as one of the bands of mustangs cross the road in front of him, the familiar chestnut stallion turning to warn the truck back with a look before following the boss mare along with the rest of them.

Patterson adjusts his ball cap on his head and watches them. There are eight total and all but the stallion are some variation of bay. After they've trotted all the way off the horizon, Patterson following them with his eyes the whole way, he catches notice of the other truck. It's parked off the side of the road just past where the horses had crossed, a Wild Mustang Mesa logo on the door. And leaning against it, Henry and Emma, watching him.

Patterson spins up alongside them and rolls down the passenger's-side window. "Was it a cold one?" he asks.

A flicker of a smile occurs somewhere in Henry's beard. He's gaunt, like the winter's whittled away at him, but he still looks all the part of rakish rodeo bum. "Not the coldest we've ever had." He tamps the ground with his cane. "But it was cold."

"The horses look good," Patterson says. "Almost wild."

Emma grins at that. She's young, just out of her teens, with a body that's a little too long to be entirely gainly. Her face is broad, broken by light freckles, and now, in the morning light, there's a blond tint to her dark red hair. She was raised on the mesa, and whatever her oddities, she's put up with Henry for more than two years now, serving as his assistant. Together they take care of the stables used by the summer vacationers and tend to the wild horses, making sure they don't get the urge to go get wild somewhere else or inconvenience anybody by dying in the middle of the road.

"Patterson's ashamed of the horses," Henry says to her. "Doesn't have a reason in the world to be, he got a hell of a deal on his cabin. But he's still ashamed of the horses."

"I think they're the best thing about living here," Emma says. She's not the kind who can hold two thoughts in her head at the same time. Who can be embarrassed at something she loves. She'll have to grow into that.

"They are," Henry says. "They're goddamn beautiful. Some people won't have nothing that ain't authentic."

"I'm gonna go open the place up," Patterson says, before the lecture begins.

"I'll be up before too long," Henry says.

Patterson nods. "Do that." He touches his hat. "Emma."

She touches her forehead, mocking him. "Patterson."

•   •   •

Homecoming. A half dozen piñon pines circle the cabin, their trunks twisted as though they've been caught trying to scuttle off the mesa without being noticed. Patterson shoulders open the heavy door, cold dust and ash whirling across the firepitted floor. Sancho snakes his way through Patterson's legs and curls up on the tattered rope rug between the small woodstove and the battered couch. You can tell he's ready to move to the cabin full-time, Sancho. He's a black and tan German shepherd mixed with something else big, a work dog, and it used to be he couldn't wait for some new disaster-ruined city to explore. But now he spends most of his time curled up behind Patterson's seat, moping for the mesa and waiting on his human to bring him food.

"Well," Patterson says to Sancho. They look at each other for a minute, then Sancho throws his head to the side and slaps his tongue out at his nose. "You missed it, didn't you?" Patterson says. Sancho snorts from somewhere deep down in his throat and puts his back to him. Sancho's a smart dog. He knows Patterson wants to talk and he's not interested.

"Fine," Patterson says. He peels off his Avrilla ball cap and tosses it on the table, following with his keys. Then he makes a piñon fire in the woodstove, and walks the food he bought out to the root cellar he made last season by burying a refrigerator under the floor in the shed. He finds canned food already in the shed that he doesn't remember buying. And a half-empty bottle of Evan Williams.

"You awake?" Patterson asks when he gets back in. Sancho doesn't answer. So Patterson sits down at the table and starts a list of what he'll need from the Walmart in Alamosa.

Then he stops writing and just sits. The last of the evening light filters in through the dusty windows. Cool valley air, the smell of burning pine. Patterson lights the kerosene lantern, sending wick light and shadow rippling across the walls.

A wind builds over the mesa. The kind of wind that whistles right through him. Outside, the piñons crackle and the brush rustles. It's a homecoming, all right. Patterson pulls out his box of pictures of his son and gets properly drunk.

half

Patterson wakes on his thin mattress in the loft to the sound of his cell phone ringing. It's just before daybreak and the phone's on the table, of course. He fumbles his way down out of the loft, banging into everything he can find a way to bang into. It's Laney on the caller ID. Which, if he'd thought about at all, he would have known before getting out of bed.

"Hello," he rasps into the phone.

"Hello, yourself," she says. "Are you settled in?"

Patterson hasn't heard her voice in almost a year, but it still washes over him like somebody's poured gasoline down his neck. "Pretty close." He makes his way to the sink, peering out the window over the hand pump. Deep darkness, the first glimmer of light barely registering. "How'd you know I was back?"

She laughs. "You're at the window, aren't you? Looking to see if I'm outside?"

"How'd you know I was back?" he asks again.

"Lucky guess," she says.

"Pretty lucky. I only pulled in this evening."

"I need to talk to you," she says. "I have a question."

"Go ahead."

"Not on the phone," she says. "I want you live and in person, so it costs you something when you give me the wrong answer. Can you come down to Taos tomorrow? I can buy you dinner."

"How's the day after tomorrow?" Patterson squints out at the morning again, still not sure she isn't out there somewhere.

"It's not something you have to prepare yourself for," she says. "It's dinner and a question."

"The day after tomorrow."

"The day after tomorrow." She sighs. "Where do you want to meet?"

"You employed?"

"I'm employed."

"The Adobe Bar," Patterson says. "Six o'clock." He ends the call.

Patterson cooks flapjacks and bacon on the woodstove, polishing off a generous glass of whiskey while he does so. Neither the bacon nor the whiskey help much with the hangover, but they give him an opportunity to enjoy one of the cabin's greatest advantages. The outhouse. Where you can take a shit with the door open, watching the morning sun wash yellow across the scrub, the prickly pear cactus trying to match its southern brothers in shadow if not substance. After breakfast, Patterson pulls on his loggers and he and Sancho take a walk on the grass-patched dirt road that runs by the cabin, Patterson hoping fresh air will cure what hair of the dog and bacon couldn't.

The morning drifts past him in a painfully bright haze. Wildflowers list purple in the light morning wind, bullet-pocked washers and refrigerators lie abandoned in the ditches. Dew mists off the mesa toward the high sun, the air bristling with morning insects. Sancho wanders ditch to ditch in broken zigzags.

Then Patterson comes around a corner and almost walks into the rear bumper of a matte-black 1969 Dodge Charger pulled off the side of the road, the driver's-side door hanging open and the door-ajar bell ringing tinnily. "Shit," Patterson says, to nobody in particular, realizing how far he'd been gone into thinking about nothing.

"That's hardly neighborly," a man's voice says. It's Henry's son, Junior. He steps around a tree, zipping up his jeans, the dust on his alligator-skin cowboy boots pocked with urine. He has a midtwenties' version of Henry's face, just as handsome but with a grin that never seems too far from a sneer and a marred left iris that's filmed over gray. He pulls a black handkerchief out of his back pocket and dabs at the eye, which seems to be perpetually weeping.

A wary growl rumbles out of Sancho's throat. Patterson crouches and strokes his neck. "Junior," Patterson says, by way of greeting.

"Patterson," Junior says in the same tone of voice. "Need a beer?"

"I could use one," Patterson says.

Junior reaches into the car and tosses him a can of Budweiser.

Patterson pops the tab, drinks.

"You always had the dog?" Junior asks.

"A few years."

"What is it?"

"Mutt. Some part German shepherd, but mostly mutt."

"He's a good-looking dog."

"Visiting Henry?" Patterson asks.

"Something like that." Junior leans back on the car, bending his head at Patterson like his neck is just a little bit broken.

"Something like what?"

Junior hacks something globular and wet up from his lungs, spits it in the dirt. "You seen him? Henry?"

"You check down at the barn?"

"I did. He ain't there."

"Probably working," Patterson says. "Might be one of the horses is sick."

"Might be," Junior says. "Might be he found him some little bitch down in San Luis that don't mind he's a cripple."

"He's allowed," Patterson says.

Junior looks off at the north. "Which one of those is the one where they found the horse?" he asks, nodding at the mountains.

"Horse?" Patterson repeats.

"Snippy," Junior says.

"It was the Blanca Massif," Patterson says. He points at the mountains on the north rim of the valley, sloping up from the floor to a sawtoothed ridge, the peaks blue-gray and snowcapped. "Can't miss 'em."

Junior squints. "Where?"

"Straight," Patterson says. "It's the five peaks right there. Little Bear, Blanca Peak, California Peak, Mount Lindsey, and Huerfano Peak."

"I heard about it on that dipshit radio show Henry listens to," Junior says. "Brother Joe. You believe all that shit he gets from that damn show?"

"Not much," Patterson says.

Junior nods for a second or two. Then he says, "Did he tell you that I gave him the money to move out here?"

"No," Patterson says. "He didn't."

"I sure enough did. Didn't have a pot to piss in and I gave him everything I had. Never saw it again, neither."

"I don't have any interest in getting in the middle of your shit," Patterson says. "None."

"Sure," Junior says. "But there's a bunch of things you ain't heard about that old asshole. Don't let him fool you none."

Patterson pours the rest of the beer in the dirt and tosses the empty can in the ditch.

Junior laughs out loud. He walks around to the driver's side of the car and climbs in, still laughing. "It's real easy to do with the second half, ain't it, partner?" he says, starting up the engine.

Justin

I don't know if I ever told you about the horse, Snippy, but that's probably the strangest story to come out of the valley. She was found in 1967, skinned nose to shoulders, completely empty of organs. Not a drop of blood, neither. The lady who owned her said she was killed by flying saucers. Said they'd be back. And, sure enough, it was only a couple years later that the cattle mutilations started. And they've been continuing off and on ever since.

I went and looked at a calf they found during the last round. Henry took me. It was in the shadow of this wind-twisted pine in the middle of a field of brown scrub. It'd been completely cored out, just a hole in the middle of the carcass where the organs had been, and its face had been cut off in laser-straight lines, not a drop of blood to be found.

Of course, some believe that there ain't really any cattle mutilations at all. Or, at least, that they aren't caused by anything as exotic as aliens. The story runs that a man from Denver named John Baylor bought a hundred thousand acres in 1960 with the intent of clear-cutting it, only to find out that the land shouldn't have been for sale. That it was communal-use land guaranteed by a Mexican land grant in 1863. Most descendants of the people who settled this valley under that original grant, they're still here. They ranch and they farm, and they have about as much interest in newcomers as they have in mosquitoes. They're transplanted Mexicans who never bothered to concern themselves with the English language or any legal niceties past what gave them their stake. Anyway, as you can imagine, they weren't real happy about land that they considered theirs being fenced in and clear-cut. So they put up a fight. There were shootouts, fires set, fences cut, beatings, the whole bit. Baylor even hired a private army.

It wasn't too long after that Snippy was found and the cattle mutilations started, with a bunch of folks saying it was aliens. Not the folks who were fighting with Baylor, though. See, they couldn't help but notice that the aliens seemed to mainly target his opponents. It drove a lot of them out of business, too. When you're a small outfit, it doesn't take the loss of too many five-thousand-dollar steers to put you under. And supposedly Brother Joe has evidence of helicopters taking off and landing at the Baylor Ranch. The fact that it would be a half century and running now, and that John Baylor's long dead and his children would have to be the ones carrying on the cattle killings, that doesn't even slow Brother Joe down. He's the kind who believes in tradition.

For my part, I don't know which sounds more far-fetched, Black Op cattle killings or aliens. Brother Joe believes in both as far as I can tell. Only last night he was on about the lights over the mountains, which he says are aliens. He says he saw one trail that ran the whole San Juan range, which'd be the whole west side of the valley, then stopped in front of Mount Blanca, and shot around the Sangre de Cristo range on the east side. All in the time it took him to smoke a cigarette. Then he started in about underground government bases and some secret tribe of wandering Jews. Which is about when I turned the radio off.

When I lived in New Mexico with you and your mother I used to drive up here a lot. Some of those trips were because I needed to get out of the house, but some were just because I needed a sunset. I read a lot about the valley before I moved here, too. One of the things about clearing power lines is that you spend a lot of time sitting in a bucket truck waiting for the work to start, and I've always spent that time reading. One thing I read is that if you ask a Navajo Indian about the valley, they'll tell you it's sacred. They'll tell you that Blanca Peak is the Dawn Mountain, and that it's strapped to the ground with lightning. Which, if you see it at sunrise, you'll understand.

6

outlaws

CO-159 is about as straight a piece of road as you can find, carving through the flat bottom of the San Luis Valley like it's been dragged into the landscape with a machete. It's the kind of highway that makes it hard not to speed, and when the gray sky's about ten feet off the ground and the sun's streaking bolts of yellow light through pinhole gaps in the firmament and raindrops are just beginning to pock your windshield, it makes it nearly impossible not to drink while you're doing it.

Not that Junior's trying real hard not to do either, running a hundred miles an hour north toward Denver with a beer between his legs, his elbow hanging out the window, empty cans and Marlboro boxes rustling around on the floorboards like there's a rat digging through them. The way he's feeling, he knows that if he weren't on a schedule, he'd end up driving loops through the valley, running himself dry of gas and beer, smoking until his lungs burned. That he'd probably find himself shivering awake into a San Luis Valley sunrise with his cowboy boots hanging out the window, the car pulled off to the side of some dirt road.

He's even thought to himself about buying some little patch of scrubland down here and building himself a cabin. But he knows better than to think he could live that close to Henry and both of them survive it. Not to mention Patterson, the sanctimonious prick.

That's the kind of fucking idiot who lives up on the mesa, Patterson. The kind who'd buy into a land scam, playing at living off the grid. Cheap plots for city fuckers who want a place in the country. They advertise it as a vacation resort, but it ain't. The roads are dirt, and half the places don't even have power. What they end up with are half-ass survivalists. Junior almost hopes that the apocalypse they're hoping for comes, just so he can drive down from Denver and shoot every one of them. Henry first.

On the north side of Denver, there's a roadhouse bar with a creek running behind it. Red trim and a red door, no windows at all, sitting off a side street in a sparsely used warehouse park. Junior spins the Charger into the gravel lot, parks in the line of motorcycles and pickup trucks. He's got the feeling full-on now. The same feeling that always shows up after visiting with his father.

It's something like trying to swallow a two-by-four. Or maybe waking up to find yourself falling out of a moving truck. It's a feeling that comes when he remembers his mother, too. When he tries to remember her face, and can't exactly. When he thinks about the days when she wasn't working and Henry was on the rodeo circuit.

She'd spend the whole day sitting in bed, smoking cigarettes. Staring at the wall like paralyzed while Junior did dishes, caught up on laundry, swept the floors. Then he'd bring her dinner, tomato soup from a can, and a seared grilled cheese sandwich, and set it down on the bed. And she'd look at the food and look at him and then her cigarette in the ashtray and pull him in for a hug, crying again. And all he could think of was how he couldn't wait for Henry to walk through the door, crowing about whatever he'd won or lost.

Inside the bar, Junior takes a stool next to a paunchy Indian woman in a leather vest and chaps. She's with a bald black biker in his thick-muscled forties. He's wearing some kind of bone hanging from his leather motorcycle jacket, a touch shared by every one of his comrades. And he's smoking a cigar. Or not so much smoking it as conducting a love affair with it. Puffing it, blowing it, working its burn as sure and steady as some long-awaited one-night stand.

Junior's never met a single biker who didn't consider himself an outlaw. Not one. And it doesn't matter that ninety-nine percent of them pay their taxes, live in a cul-de-sac, and wouldn't say boo to a cop if he was raping them with his nightstick. Granted, there's the other one percent, and Junior's even tangled with a few known to run a little crank, but they don't impress him. The way he figures it, bikers are just about as much outlaws as rodeo riders are cowboys.

"Bourbon. A big glass," Junior says to the bartender. He looks at the Indian woman. "You got a name?"

"Janet." She doesn't look at him.

"An Indian name," Junior says.

Now she looks at him. "An Indian name?"

Junior pulls out his handkerchief and dabs his bad eye with it. "Dances with Niggers, maybe?"

creek

Junior drools blood into the creek. The middle of the creek where he's standing. He tries to spit, but he drools instead. Shards of tooth slip out over his swollen lip with the blood. The middle of a creek. He's got the feeling he's coming awake out of a very hard sleep. The tendons in his left arm sing a strained and painful note, and there's a hard chord of nausea that cuts through him when he breathes.

It's raining, he thinks very clearly. He can hear the raindrops pattering around him in the creek water. But he can also see the stars and moon spinning over him, tilt-a-whirling. And there are the lights of Denver, orange through the cottonwoods and creek willows. He touches his head and realizes it's not rain at all he's hearing. It's blood, pouring from his head down into the black water.

He can hear something else, too. Something happening not too far down. It sounds like a party and there's a kind of light wavering through the cottonwoods. A strange smoking yellow by the bank, ringed by shadowy figures. Some of them capering in the flame and smoke, and some just standing there seeming to smoke as if on fire themselves. He takes a step toward them.

"I wouldn't do that, motherfucker," a voice calls out from the light.

Junior's not sure what it is he shouldn't do. He takes another step, against the current, the creek sucking at his boot. Before he can find footing on the bottom, a rock plugs him directly on top of the head, dropping him to his knees like he's been hit on the point of his skull with a ball-peen hammer. Another rock plunks down a foot to the left of him. A third splashes his face with creek water.

He tries to stand, can't make it. Another rock hits him in his shoulder, a repulsive jolt jamming up his arm like he's grabbed on to an electric line. He scrabbles for the bank, his hands and feet slipping. His right hand goes out from under him, his elbow slamming down on a stone. Pain rips up his forearm, explodes in his fingertips. He scrambles up the creek bank, through a stand of creek willows, collapses.

He does all he can to not pass out.

It's not enough.

bathtubs

The sun sends yellow runners of light streaking across the creek's surface like water bugs, and Junior sits up and vomits into his lap. Then, when he's sure he's done, he takes off his brand-new alligator-skin cowboy boots and dumps the filthy water. Then peels off his socks and squeezes them out. He has to do it one-handed, because he can't raise his left arm, the shoulder useless. And every time he moves his head the vision in his good eye washes away and he has to force back another round of retching.

He doesn't know which looks worse, his feet or the boots. So he doesn't think about it. He rinses his mouth out with creek water. Then somehow stands and hunches his way back toward the road-house. For some reason walking down the middle of the creek instead of along the bank, staggering out of the mud like some new species of amphibian monster, making his way through the empty parking lot.

He passes the still-smoking corpse of his 1969 Charger. Thinking what a goddamn good thing it is that he made this particular trip down to the San Luis Valley on his own time. That he wasn't stopped on his way back from a run down to El Paso for Vicente. That would not have been a loss he's entirely sure he would have survived.

It's the same bartender as last night. A ruddy middle-aged man in a fringed buckskin shirt, reading a tabloid newspaper behind the bar. "I'll be damned," he says, when Junior takes a stool at the bar. "I thought you were dead."

"Give it a little time," Junior says. "The matter ain't entirely settled yet."

The bartender pours a beer glass half-full of bourbon and hands it to him. Then he leans on the bar, watching Junior as if he might do some new trick. Sprout flowers from his head, maybe. Or spontaneously combust. "Did they do that to your eye?" he asks.

Junior shakes his head, holding the glass of whiskey. It's not often he's scared of a glass of whiskey, but he's a little scared of this one. "What time is it?"

"Four o'clock in the afternoon. You just now waking up?"

Junior takes a drink of the whiskey and it hurts just as much as he thought it would. "Yep."

"Where you live?"

"Forty-seventh and Vine."

"That's got to be five miles. How you going to get home?"

"I ain't thought it through yet."

"You ain't got anyone you can call?"

"Who would you want to tell this story to?" Junior asks.

The bartender nods at that, fingering a Camel cigarette out of a pack on the bar. "You know, I had a wife once," he says. "I caught her with a nigger."

"I'd be careful who I commented on it to, partner." Junior makes a point of not smiling when he says it.

The bartender lights his cigarette. "They weren't fucking neither. My wife and the nigger."

Junior takes another drink of the whiskey. It doesn't hurt nearly as bad this time. "You got an extra one of those?"

The bartender slides the pack to him. "Keep it."

Junior lights up, wincing at the pain that shoots through his head as he draws smoke. He pulls the cigarette out of his mouth. Blood on the filter.

"He was pissing on her, is what he was doing." The bartender clears his throat. "They'd been doing it for more'n a year before I caught on."

"Pissing on her?"

"Pissing on her."

"Seems like that wouldn't be a hard one to catch on to," Junior says. "Seems like you'd notice the wet spots around the house. Maybe smell it."

The bartender nods his head. "They did it in the tub, mainly," he says. "They met on the computer. Turns out there's whole groups of people for that kind of shit."

"You can find most anything on computers these days," Junior says.

"It wasn't just him, neither." The bartender pours himself a bourbon. "I mean it was only niggers. Just not always the same one. That's what she told me. She could only get off if the guy pissing on her was black."

"She told it to you?"

"Yeah. I asked her why she didn't just let me piss on her instead."

Junior folds a cocktail napkin into quarters and holds it on his dead eye. Then he barks out a single laugh.

The bartender's face reddens. He doesn't look at Junior. "I just mean I can give you a ride home," he says.

Junior crumples up the napkin and drops it on the bar, then holds up his fist. "Solidarity, brother."

drunk

It's only after the bartender pulls away that Junior realizes he doesn't have his house key. And that he already knew that. That his house key has gone the same way as his wallet and cell phone. He stands on the porch cursing himself for a fucking idiot for maybe two minutes, then stumbles off, finds a hunk of blacktop in the gutter, and walks it back up to the door, his head plunked down in his shoulders like he's been hit over the crown with a sledgehammer. But just before he chunks the asphalt through the window he stops, a rare moment of reflection passing over him. Knowing the last thing he wants to do is spend the next day caulking in new glass. So he drops it and walks up to Forty-seventh, toward Jenny's. It's ramshackle houses and chain-link fences and the occasional chicken coop, and it's dark enough that it looks almost like any other working-class neighborhood in Denver. The houses a little smaller than most, sure, but at least you can't see the way the vinyl siding's peeling from the combined fumes of the oil refinery, rendering plant, and dog food factory. And it's late enough that most everybody is off their porch. Or at least those that aren't know Junior well enough to keep from doing anything that might get his attention at this time of night.

Jenny opens her bedroom window right away when he taps, like she's been sitting up waiting for him to stop by. Which, maybe she has. A smile takes ten years off her battered face, some of the bags and lumps disappearing as shadows, those still left unable to crowd out the weary good looks that remain. But the smile flashes away like heat lightning when she gets a better look at him. "I'll meet you at the front door," she says.

She's sitting on the stoop with two bottles of Budweiser in her lap when he comes around the house. "Do I even want to ask?" She lights a menthol cigarette and squints through the smoke at his face.

He sits down next to her. "I went up to see Henry."

"Run into a rugby team on your way back?"

He grunts something that isn't quite a laugh.

"You want to be careful with that face," she says. "It's pretty much all you got going for you."

"Except for the eye," he says.

"Nobody minds the eye but you."

He shrugs. "I don't think anything's broken. Maybe a tooth or two."

The smoke from her cigarette wisps into her eyes. She waves her hand at it. "So you know, I can't fuck you," she says. "I'm on my period."

Junior stands and walks around the side of her house.

"What are you doing?" she asks.

"You got any plans tomorrow?" Junior asks, unzipping his pants.

"No," she says. "Tell me you're not pissing against the side of my house."

Junior answers her by pissing against the side of her house.

"I've got a bathroom. It's about ten feet from you right now."

Junior returns to the stoop, standing. "Mind driving me to a car lot in the morning?"

"I probably don't want to ask, do I?"

"Probably not," he says. "Also, I lost my house key. I need yours."

"Am I getting it back?"

He holds out his hand.

She pulls her keys out of her pocket, strips his house key off the ring, and hands it to him. "You can stay for a little while if you want," she says. "I got a joint."

"I'm drunk." He sways a little when he says it.

"That's never stopped you from anything I ever heard of. You at least wanna look in on Casey?"

"I don't wanna wake her up."

"You won't. She sleeps like me, not you."

"Not tonight."

She lowers her head a little to take another drag off her cigarette, and she doesn't look back up at him. He knows it's because she doesn't want him to see whatever she's thinking. And, as always, that makes him wish he was just about anywhere else. So he walks to the gate.

"I really do like your face," she says to his back. "Try taking a little care of it for me, if nothing else."

whiskey

Whoever built the cabin had the sense to set it facing the Blanca Massif, which is pretty much the only criteria Patterson had when he bought it. Right now he's on his porch, just finishing watching the first sunset of the season play over the west side of Mount Blanca, when Henry pulls into the driveway. He climbs out of his truck and, holding on to the doorframe, fumbles his cane out from behind the driver's seat. "Sieg Heil," he calls, rollicking his way up to the porch.

"Cut that shit out," Patterson says. He stands and takes Henry's arm, helping him up the crooked steps.

Henry hangs his cane over the porch rail and sinks down in one of the camp chairs. "Where's that bachelor mutt of yours?" he asks.

"I don't know." Patterson peers out into the gloom for a second. "He ain't been back all day."

"Probably found himself a little bitch," Henry says.

Patterson looks at him.

"Right." Henry chuckles.

"I found a bottle of whiskey in the outhouse. You want a glass?"

"Whiskey in the shitter," Henry says admiringly. "How many exactly would you say you've got stashed away around here?"

"It ain't entirely his fault," Henry says later, much later. They've let the kerosene lantern run out of fuel hours ago, and the stars are so numerous and low you could soak your feet in them.

"Which part?" Patterson asks.

"The part about him hating my guts." Henry's holding on to the hook of his cane with both hands, resting his chin on it. "I wasn't around much, and it'd probably have been better if I hadn't been when I was."

"You were hard on him?"

"I was a sorry son of a bitch." Henry leans forward toward the darkness. "There. I thought I saw something move."

"Where?"

"Past my truck."

Patterson narrows his eyes and tries to stare himself sober. Then he spots it, a quick dog-sized hole in the darker darkness. "That's Sancho." Patterson leans back in his chair.

"Why ain't he coming in?" Henry asks.

"He's embarrassed."

Henry chuckles. "He's got a lot of personality, your dog."

Patterson raises two fingers to his mouth and blows a loud whistle. Sancho's head raises. "Can I ask you a question?" Patterson asks Henry.

"I don't think he's coming," Henry remarks.

"SANCHO," Patterson yells. "GET YOUR ASS UP HERE." His voice sounds strained and weak in his ears, like it's coming from an accordion with torn bellows. But the dog rises to his feet and mopes toward the porch.

"What was the question?" Henry asks.

Sancho slinks warily up the steps, making as if to head through the flap in the front door. Patterson grabs him by the skin of his neck and yanks him yelping by his leg. "Did he give you the money to move out here?"

Henry barked a laugh. "I was only coming from Cheyenne. He loaned me two hundred bucks for gas. I paid that off with my first paycheck."

Patterson pats Sancho down for injury. Nothing but mud and burrs. He scratches Sancho's head with one hand, strokes his neck with the other. Then he puts his face into Sancho's neck and holds it there. Sancho smells wild and happy. Happy to be wild, and happy to be home from it. "He says otherwise."

"Yeah?" says Henry. "Well. He may even believe it."

lemonade

The Adobe Bar is the hotel bar for the Taos Inn, right downtown in tourist central, modeled on the real Taos Pueblo where the Pueblo Indians have lived for more than a thousand years. It has a neon thunderbird sign out front and hosts new age flute players most weekend nights, but if you can stand all that there's every kind of bourbon you could want. And that had seemed pretty important to Patterson when Laney had said she needed to talk to him.

She's already seated at a table. She looks good, too good. At least ten years younger than Patterson. Which is not exactly some great feat, but is still no fun to look at. She's lost weight and replaced it with lean muscle, and her broad Irish face has mellowed some, either because of her age or because of something she's had done to it. Whatever it is, it's softened some of her shrill edges, and almost gives her the illusion of tenderness.

And then there's the little boy with her, her new son, Gabe. He's three years old now, sucking the sugary life out of a tall glass of pink lemonade next to her. Patterson tries not to stare holes in his face while Laney makes small talk.

How are you doing, Patterson? Still living up on that mesa so you don't have to be around people? Still drinking yourself stupid every night? Still don't have the guts to settle down and live like an adult?

None of which is said, exactly, just implied. But, then, she's always been very good at implication.

Finally, just before Patterson excuses himself for the bathroom to hang himself with his belt, she comes to the point. "I have a lawyer," she says.

Patterson is still staring at the boy when she says it. Trying hard not to, but still staring.

"You can talk to him, Patterson." Her voice softens in a way that makes Patterson even more uncomfortable than he already is. "Say hello, Gabe," she says to the boy. "This is Patterson. Patterson Wells. Do you remember him from last summer?"

Gabe wrinkles his nose, grinning with his lips puckered around his straw. Patterson finishes his first bourbon double and thanks Jesus he had the sense to order himself two.

"He remembers you," Laney says. "He always remembers men. I think it's because his father isn't around."

Patterson clears his throat, but he has nothing.

"They finally got him," she says. "He burnt his house down trying to make meth. He never was very good at following recipes." She smiles at Patterson. "We were never together, not really. But you know that."

Patterson doesn't know that. He's never met Gabe's father. Whatever happened between them had happened while he was on the road. He just came back after a season of work one year and she was pregnant. But he nods like he knows the whole story, mainly so she doesn't tell it to him again.

Laney rubs Gabe's shoulder. "It was worth it," she says. The way the boy's going at his lemonade, you'd think it'd take him two seconds to finish it, but the level of the liquid barely seems to move.

"You got a lawyer," Patterson prompts. Gabe's one thing he can't talk about for any length of time.

"I have a lawyer," she says. "He's seen the medical records and he thinks we have a case."

"A case of what?"

"A lawsuit, Patterson," she says. "A lawsuit against Dr. Court for what he did to Justin. For letting him die. We're not the only ones. He has no right to hold a license. What he likes is looking like a doctor. Having everybody impressed with him for it. But he's messed up all kinds of people. Justin was the only one he killed, but he messed up others. Other kids."

"You got a lawyer," Patterson repeats.

"I want to add you as a plaintiff," she says. "That's what I wanted to talk to you about."

Patterson shakes his head.

"You don't have to pay anything," she says. "All you have to do is sign a piece of paper."

Patterson continues to shake his head.

"If somebody doesn't stop him, there's no reason to think he won't do it again. That other parents won't have to go through exactly what we did."

Patterson is still shaking his head.

"Okay," she says. "Let's try this. It's money. Not a little money, a lot of money. You're too old for the work you do. You were too old when we met, now you're too old by ten years. Do you have a retirement plan?"

"I've got the cabin," Patterson says.

"The cabin," she repeats in a voice that makes it easy to tell she doesn't think much of the cabin as a retirement plan. She fixes Patterson in place with her brown eyes, smirking so imperceptibly you could almost miss it. "I won't give up on this," she says. "I can be persistent. And you can't keep doing what you're doing."

Patterson doesn't say anything, and he doesn't bother shaking his head again. There are plenty of advantages to being married, though he could never properly enumerate them, but the biggest advantage to not being married is not having to explain yourself. Sometimes Patterson even remembers that in time to keep from doing it.

"Well," she says brightly, "are you ready to order food?"

"I've gotta get back to Sancho," Patterson lies. "He ain't feeling good."

"Sancho," she says. "I miss Sancho."

"He's a good dog." It comes out warbly. Patterson clears his throat.

"Does he still hate women?"

"Everyone but you," Patterson says.

"He's a dog with sense," she says. "I'd like to see him."

Patterson nods and finishes his second bourbon. Then he pats her on the shoulder and walks out. It's probably the cruelest thing he can do, given what she's asking him. But it's either that or grab her by her carefully piled hair and start pounding her face into the table.

chess

It took Junior a while to recover, but he finally did. After a couple of days of not moving much at all, he took a bath in his big claw-foot tub, the water near to boiling. The muscles and tendons stretched out in the heat, and it looked like the only real injury he'd sustained was two broken molars. That and the loose canine. And the black eye and swollen nose. And the lips that could do decent work as sausage models. But nothing that wouldn't heal given a little time. Junior remembers Henry coming home after rodeos looking worse. Sometimes after he'd won, even. And sometimes when he hadn't ridden.

The real problem was that Junior couldn't find another 1969 Charger anywhere. He and Jenny had looked all day, rolling from car lot to car lot, Casey tagging along, offering her input on the matter. That one's pink, Daddy, get that one. Get that one, Daddy, it's got fuzzy dice. If you get that one we can go camping, Daddy.

My friend Alicia went camping with her daddy, and they caught six fish. They had to let them all go, though. But if you buy that one I'll bet we could catch twice as many, and I get sick of her bragging.

But nothing would do for Junior but to get something as close to his original car as he could find, and that turned out to be a 1972 Charger with a new engine. The only hitch being that it was lime green. So, after counting his cash into the salesman's hand, Junior drove it straight off the lot to a Mexican body shop by his house to get it painted black.

He's heard all the arguments against driving conspicuous vehicles in his line of work. He knows other drivers who make it a point to never drive anything but minivans and sedans. But Junior, he doesn't figure there's any point in being a drug runner if you can't drive a cool car.

Of course, not an hour after he got home from picking the freshly painted car up from the body shop, he got a call from Vicente. It was the first of several, which is always the way it happens. Six trips down to El Paso in three days. I-25 both ways, the endless interstate blur. No time for sleep or even a sit-down meal.

Now that he's back home on the couch and trying to nap through the morning sun, Junior's lower back feels like some small animal's made a nest in it and is trying to gnaw its way out. He's not complaining, though. Sure as hell not to Vicente.

Before Vicente, Junior had no prospects at all. After his mother died, he'd been run straight into foster homes, Henry making no attempt to hang on to him at all. They weren't the kind of foster homes you hear about, the bad ones. When Junior was younger and drunk in the Colfax bars he would tell people they were, but they weren't. He just had to say something about the shit Henry had piled up in his head, and none of what was real seemed like enough. Henry wasn't the first father who wasn't much of one, and Junior wasn't the first boy to ever grow up in foster care. But it was the only childhood Junior'd ever had, and he needed it to sound as lonesome and dangerous as he felt it.

Still, life in a foster home hadn't left him with a lot of preparation for the job market. And he'd never been very interested in the education side of school. So he left the last home when he was seventeen and started working day labor with Mexicans, falling in and out of weekly rooms on Colfax. Fistfighting the cowboys who stayed in those hotels when the rodeo was in town, getting drunk alone in his room or outside in the parks.

That's where he met Vicente, in a park. He was setting up chess problems for himself at a picnic table and Junior was spread out on a bench, working off a hangover with the spring sun and a bottle of fortified wine. Chess was the only thing Henry'd ever taught Junior. On those warm afternoons he couldn't afford a bar, which were many, Henry'd brown-bag a bottle of wine down to one of the picnic tables on the St. Vrain River that cuts through Longmont, carrying his pieces in a grocery sack and taking all comers, playing Junior in between money games.

Henry played a looping and erratic game that he learned from other rodeo riders, striking out and withdrawing in strange patterns that defied recognition, and he'd taught Junior the same. Their first game, Vicente checkmated Junior in eleven moves. They played six more games after that, all of which Vicente won easily. But when they were done Vicente asked Junior a few questions, then offered him a job driving. At the time, Junior was working twelve-hour days delivering sandstone to construction sites. He accepted on the spot.

• • •

The knocking hits like a midnight hailstorm, rattling Junior awake so abruptly that he falls off the couch in a flurry, striking out at the air to clutch anything that might stop his fall. "What?" he yells.

The knocking continues. Junior smoothes down his T-shirt, answers the door. It's Jenny, in a clean pantsuit that has a worn Goodwill look to it. "Good morning," she says brightly. "I need a favor."

"We've all got needs," Junior says. "I need some more fucking sleep."

"It's ten o'clock in the morning."

"I was driving all night. Didn't get back until seven."

"Casey's in the car," she says. "I need you to watch her."

"I'm fucking tired."

"Please," she says. "I've got a job interview."

"What do you mean, job interview?"

"Typing. Data entry."

"If you need money, tell me you need money."

"It's at the Tech Center and Mom's sick. Three hours tops. Please."

Junior presses his bad eye against his shoulder. "All right. Send her in."

"Thank you." She kisses him quickly on the cheek and turns to run down the porch steps, but stops. "Do you need a couple of minutes to clean up anything? Put anything away?"

"I've been on the road," Junior says. "Ain't nothing she can get into."

Jenny starts to say something else, standing on the top step. Then she bites her bottom lip.

"What?" Junior says.

"Can you put on your eye patch?" she says. "It scares her."

stink

Junior lives in the battered residential neighborhood of Elyria-Swansea, tucked away in the junkyards, body shops, and crumbling beer joints of Northeast Denver. It has the distinction of being within two miles of six Superfund sites, one of which happens to be the neighborhood itself. When the stink of oil and animal waste being processed rolls in on a hot afternoon it's a little like being suffocated in sewage. They call it the big stink, and rumor has it that you can get used to it after a while. That third-generation residents have even been known to claim they can't smell it at all. But there are very few third-generation residents left.

It does have a few advantages over the rest of Denver, though, and one of them is its lack of police presence, which Junior decidedly enjoys. In every city there are neighborhoods abandoned to industry. Wastelands and disaster zones sacrificed to the greater good. As long as you can stand to live in them, they're one of the few places you can almost be free to be left alone.

Today the stink isn't too bad, so Junior and his daughter sit on the front porch on kitchen chairs. They'd been inside, but she'd brought a DVD of *The Wizard of Oz*, and the absence of a television had set her crying. Junior's pretty sure he used to have a television, a little color model, but it's sure as hell gone. Somewhere.

"Do you know why they call the lion the Cowardly Lion?" Casey asks. Her feet don't reach the ground. She swings them back and forth, banging her dirty pink tennis shoes on the chair legs.

Junior tries not to scowl. She doesn't let anything go. "Because he's a coward," he answers her.

"Yeah," she says, as if that was a stupid answer. Which, Junior knows, it was. "But do you know why he's a coward?"

She's a little woman, all right. There's no answer that'll satisfy her but exactly the one she's looking for. "No idea," Junior says. He picks at the cuticle on his thumb. He picks too hard and his thumb rims with blood, so he sticks it in his mouth and waits for her to say something else.

"It's because he's scared of everything," she says.

"That's what coward means," Junior says. He wipes his thumb on his jeans and adjusts his eye patch. His eye sweats under it, which is part of why he doesn't wear the goddamn thing.

"I know. That's what I said."

Too smart for her age. "We should do something," Junior says. "Walk over to the park, maybe."

"I know what we should do," she says.

Junior opens his eyes. They'd closed by themselves. "What's that?"

"Maybe, just maybe, we could go to Funtastic Fun."

"I don't think so."

"Okay. It was maybe."

"It's too far for me to drive right now."

"It's okay. We can go to McDonald's instead."

Junior looks over at her. She grins at him. "You want a pop?" he asks.

"Am I allowed?"

"You're allowed if I say you're allowed."

"As long as it doesn't have caffeine. I don't want caffeine."

"I'll check."

In the kitchen, Junior opens the refrigerator and pulls a can of Big K orange soda. He lifts up his eye patch, wipes the sweat off his eye, and squints at the ingredient list. No caffeine. He sets it down, then taps a quick pile of cocaine out of his pocket vial onto the counter, and snorts it through a dollar bill, unchopped. When he raises up off the counter, he can hear her talking, faintly. "I'm going to be in first grade," she's saying. "That's why. I was in kindergarten last year."

Then a boy's voice. "Yeah, well, I get tired of it. That's all I'm saying. Fuck them."

Junior leaves the cocaine and walks out on the porch. The boy's maybe fourteen or fifteen, hunched on an idling neon-green pocket bike.

"How's about you ride off my lawn and I don't ever catch you talking to my daughter again," Junior says to him.

"I ain't on your lawn," the boy says, his lip curling. "I'm on the sidewalk. You ain't got shit to say about what I do on the sidewalk."

Junior steps off the porch after him, his hand reaching for the Glock at the small of his back without his even having thought about it. The boy kicks the miniature motorcycle into gear and scoots away down the sidewalk, jumping the curb onto the street, flashing the finger over his shoulder. "Motherfucker," Junior says under his breath. He walks back up the steps, picks up the can of soda, cracks it, and hands it to his daughter.

"He was saying some bad words," Casey says.

"I need a fence." Junior sits.

"You've got a fence out back."

"There ain't nowhere to sit out back."

She's holding the can of soda in both hands. She takes a drink. Her lips are wet and orange when she pulls the can away from her mouth. "Can I ask you a question?"

"Sure."

"What's that word?"

"What word?"

"The one you said." She watches him intently. He doesn't know how she ended up with blue eyes, but they're as blue as the Blue Lakes under Mount Blanca, and about the same size. "Mudfucker."

Junior coughs into his fist. Then lifts his eye patch and wipes his eye with his handkerchief. "Don't say that."

"What's it mean?"

"It doesn't mean anything. It's something people say when they get mad. But don't you say it."

"It's a bad word?"

"It's a bad word."

"I know fucker is a bad word. I never heard mudfucker."

"Shut up," Junior says, but he can't help grinning. "Your mother's going to kill me."

"That's a bad word, too," she says. "Shut up."

recognition

Later, after Jenny has come and picked up Casey, Junior takes his chessboard over to Vicente's and they play a game in his garage. It's one of the battered brick warehouses that litter North Denver, waiting to be set on fire or turned into a Nazi-cold meth lab. It stands back a hundred yards from the road in a field of tall grass and scrub brush, more of a compound than a home, surrounded by a chain-link fence and a barricade of used tires and rusted-out cars.

Vicente bought it when he first emigrated from El Salvador with his wife and her brother. His plan was to start an auto body shop. It was a plan that died when his wife contracted lockjaw, scraping herself on a bolt while she and Vicente pulled the abandoned wreckage out of the garage. That's as much as Junior knows. That, and that the irony of having escaped the death squads of El Salvador to lose his wife to a rusty nail did not escape Vicente.

Behind them, the brother of Vicente's wife, Eduardo, is digging under the hood of Vicente's Lexus RXH. His back is almost as wide as the chassis, his tattoos melting in and out of the shadows cast by the shop light and hood. Vicente has made comments once or twice as to how much Eduardo looks like his deceased wife. Junior is kind enough to never reflect on what that must have meant for the poor woman.

"Is that your move?" Vicente asks Junior.

Junior takes his hand off his bishop. "That's it."

"There are worse moves," Vicente says.

"I know."

"There are better moves as well."

"I figured." Junior's stupefied with exhaustion, counting the hours until dusk, letting the cocaine run out of his system. He can barely track the game at all. He's running on pattern recognition that doesn't even register in his conscious mind.

Vicente removes his round glasses, breathes on them, and wipes them on his T-shirt. His small eyes twitch, blink. "I am thinking of going back to cocaine," he says.

"No money in it," Junior says. "That's what you told me."

"There's money in it. There's not as much money in it. Not as many people have the money to afford cocaine in these economic times. Crystal meth is a workingman's drug."

"Then why go back to cocaine?"

"I don't like these methamphetamine dealers. I don't trust them. They are not like the cocaine cartels. They are not interested in drugs, they are interested in movements. They build schools and roads."

"I don't give a shit what I'm driving," Junior says.

"Can you quit snorting the cocaine?" Vicente asks.

"I have to quit snorting cocaine to drive it?"

"It is a good practice."

"You mean don't get high on your own supply?"

"Exactly." Vicente nods. "From the movie. It is a good practice."

"It's a movie," Junior says. "A Hollywood movie with Al Pacino in it. Who gives a shit what Al Pacino thinks?"

Vicente ponders that. Then he nods again. "True," he says. "But it still seems like a good practice."

Eduardo walks up behind Vicente and puts one of his huge hands on Vicente's shoulder. He has a long ponytail, and even as old as he is, it's still jet black. "Did you move?" he asks Junior.

"I moved," Junior says.

"You could have forked him with your knight. There, and there."

"I saw it."

"You saw it when?"

"Right after I moved."

Eduardo laughs out loud. "I have to make a parts run," he says to Vicente, nodding back at the Lexus. "I'll be back in an hour."

"Food," Vicente says. "Pick up some food. Chinese."

Eduardo nods and leaves them to their game.

"So what do you have against building roads, anyway?" Junior asks. "Or schools? What's wrong with schools?"

Vicente's eyes are on the board. "I don't trust movements. I've soured on movements. There is one cartel for methamphetamines now and it is a religious movement. They carry bibles of their own sayings."

"What kind of sayings?"

"A man must get his heart back. We have been wounded so deeply, we don't want our heart anymore. They have stripped us of our courage, they have destroyed our creativity, they have made intimacy with God impossible for us. We live in a love story in the midst of war. That kind. Gibberish."

"You don't believe in God?" Junior asks.

"Of course not," Vicente says.

"All right."

"You do?"

"Yeah. I don't know. Yeah."

"When you think about it, you mean."

"Yeah. When I think about it."

"Then you don't believe in God."

Junior shrugs. "All right."

Vicente moves a pawn. "How is your daughter?"

"She's all right."

"All right, all right," Vicente says. "Everything is all right with you."

"Everything's all right with me."

Vicente's cell phone rings. He takes it out of his pocket and looks at it. Then he opens it and puts it to his ear. He doesn't talk, and after a minute he closes it.

"Can you make a drive?"

Junior looks at him.

Junior doesn't mean to pull off I-25 in Walsenburg. He's snorting cocaine straight out of the vial now, drinking gas station coffee laced with bourbon. Anything to stay awake. He knows he shouldn't be adding time to the trip. Least of all pulling his wheel toward the San Luis Valley. But when you go long enough without sleep, and you're running on cocaine and fumes, your hands sort of do things of their own accord.

Justin

I still needed to make the trip to Walmart. If I'd had any sense at all I'd have just stopped in Taos after meeting your mother. But the last thing I could deal with right then was more people, and I wasn't up to facing any this morning, either. When I can find anything else to do besides going into town, I do it. So I packed the truck and drove down to the reservoir.

It was well before sunrise. I took my first drink out of the Evan Williams bottle when I climbed in the canoe, the second while waiting for Sancho's wild swim and scrabble as he clambered aboard, and a third watching the quick twittering of a foreclosure of bank swallows as they fluttered over the water to escape his splashing.

There's places all around the reservoir you can't get to easily without a canoe. I paddled for one of those places, keeping the light of the mesa's lodge and boathouse directly behind me. It was impossible to judge my progress or speed in the early morning darkness, the canoe skimming along, trying to slip right out from under me. I didn't have any idea we were to the other side until I grated to a hard stop on the bank.

I'd judged right, though, and there was the stump. It was like some half-sunken body trying to wrestle free of its own burial, covered in fresh hoof marks. I'm always surprised there are any minerals left, given how little I refresh it. I pulled the two fifty-pound sacks of mineral salt out of the canoe and emptied them over what was left of the stump. Then I hunkered down and had another drink of whiskey. Sancho shivering against my leg, still wet from climbing in and out of the canoe.

Most years I take at least one deer. Some summers I don't buy meat at all. Henry keeps it in the lodge's freezer, eating as much as he wants by way of payment. I sat and watched the morning break on that old rotted stump, half-annihilated by the hooves of deer. The sun slipped over it like morning clothes, making its old shadows and gnarls fresh and bright. I pulled from the bottle of Evan Williams and just watched. Beyond the stump, the reservoir water shimmered in slivers of ink and new-risen light. I was still nipping on the bottle. It was a beautiful morning, and it's human nature to try to improve on beauty when you can.

Besides which, I still wasn't over the work season. It used to be I'd get a night or two's worth of sleep and I'd be good to go after it was done, but these days it's a couple of weeks letting the torn muscles and stretched tendons repair. It'll build up in you, what my kind of work does to your body. I can only wonder if I'll be able to move at all in another ten years. And Avrilla, they don't bother with amenities like health insurance. Unless you need to get a hand sewn on after a chain-saw mishap, you might never see a doctor. But drinking helps. So I try not to worry about how much I'm drinking while I wait out the worst of it.

I took lunch with Sancho curled up at my feet, eating jerky out of my hand. It was exactly what I needed, sitting there, and there was no hint of your mother in the brush or in my head.

There was you. You're always there. But for at least a minute or two your mother was completely and blessedly gone.

scabs

Patterson drives the long way back from the Walmart in Alamosa, his truck bed full of supplies. After salting the stump, he hadn't been able to think of anything left to avoid town with this morning. He drives past side roads flicking away to bleak little clusters of trailers. Over a cattle guard into ranchland, through ranging beef cows as alien in the greasewood and sagebrush as water buffalo. Smoking cigarettes and watching a bank of clouds form in the gray sky, long streaks of rain striking down on the western rim of the valley. Watching those clouds darken from gray to black.

It's about two miles outside of San Luis that he runs across the Wild Mustang Mesa four-wheeler, abandoned by the side of the road, smoke pouring out of it. Patterson parks the truck and is walking back to take a look when Emma pulls up in the Wild Mesa Mustang truck behind him. "Is he here?" she asks, running to him.

"Not as far as I can tell," Patterson says.

"Did you come from San Luis or from the mesa?"

"From Alamosa, through San Luis."

Her face fell. "He must've already been to town then."

"What's going on?"

She hands Patterson a piece of paper. In a childlike scrawl, Henry's handwriting, is a note. "Gone to San Luis for beer. Start work without me." Patterson laughs once, folds it back up, and gives it back to her.

"What are you laughing at?" she snaps.

"That he left you a note," Patterson says. "That he couldn't just go get beer, but had to tell you that's what he was doing."

"You know how he gets when he drinks," she says. "He doesn't have any business going after beer."

"Hop in my truck," Patterson says. "Between the both of us, we can probably wrestle a Budweiser away from a cripple."

She gives him a dirty look, but opens the door.

They find him about a mile on, caning his way toward the mesa with a twelve-pack of beer under his arm, road dust drifting up his scuffed cowboy boots. Patterson gestures for Emma to roll down her window. "Want a ride?" he asks.

Henry's head burrows into his shoulders. He starts caning faster.

Patterson touches the gas, keeping pace with him.

"You could smoke cigarettes if you got in the truck," Emma pleads.

"I can smoke while I'm walking," Henry says.

Emma starts to say something else, but Patterson puts his finger to his lips and winks at her. "Your choice," Patterson says. They idle along next to him.

It takes a hundred yards or so, but Henry finally stops. "God-damn it."

Patterson touches the brakes. "You ain't got to stop, I got all the time in the world."

"Goddamn it," Henry says again. His hair is windswept and gritty, hovering in the coming storm. Rain begins to pock the dirt.

Emma gets out and walks toward him. "Let me help you."

He turns toward her. Congealed blood cakes the right side of his face, dull and black.

Emma stops so quick that she skids on the soles of her shoes. "Henry," she says, stepping back from him.

"Emma," he mimics her.

Emma swallows. And instead of saying whatever she'd been going to, she takes him by the arm and helps him into the truck. The clouds bulge overhead and off in the distance the sun suddenly cuts through in guillotines of light. Then the rain hits them in a torrent.

They drive Henry back to the barn, where they sit in the loft around the tack trunk that he uses for a table, twilight falling, the rain gone just as quick as it had come. Lights from the lakehouses mottle the banks of the reservoir through the window. Up at Patterson's cabin, it's like living on some deserted crater on the moon. But from Henry's loft, the mesa actually looks like the vacation spot it claims to be.

"Well," Patterson says. He wants a cigarette but is holding off on lighting one, taking in the smell of pine chips and alfalfa.

"Well," Henry mocks. He tips his beer can up over his mouth and empties it. He looks like he's been beat with a fence post. There's coagulated blood all over the side of his face, and some kind of yellow scab on his cheekbone, like a portion of his skin has been removed with a cheese grater. Still, he seems to be enjoying the attention, the smile lines around his eyes deepening.

"All right," Patterson says. "Any reason I shouldn't run up to Denver and stomp a mudhole in his ass?"

Emma starts in her chair. "Stomp a mudhole in what?" She turns to Henry. "You didn't fall off the four-wheeler?"

Henry grins blood and scabs. It would look grotesque on anyone else, but on him it manages to look a little dashing. "Do you know what he does for a living?" he says to Patterson. "My boy?"

"I got a guess," Patterson says.

Emma looks from Patterson to Henry and back again. She can't close her mouth. "It was your son?"

Henry looks out the window as if only just managing to maintain control of his emotions. He presents them with his profile.

"Why didn't you stop him?" Emma asks him.

His lower jaw works back and forth like it's slightly dislocated from the top and he's trying to reset it. "I owe him money."

"You owe him money," she repeats.

Henry drinks and then wipes beer out of his mustache. "Thanks for giving me a ride home," he says.

"But now you want us to leave you here," Emma says. "Well, I'm not leaving. I'm not going back to my trailer and leaving you here like this." She crosses her arms. And then she stuffs one fist in her mouth and stares at the window.

Patterson stands. "We'll check on you tomorrow," he says. "Come on, Emma."

debts

Junior's out in his backyard, cutting treated pine boards to size with a circular saw. He's hired two local alcoholic rednecks to help him with the deck, and he's regretting it already. The frame is many things, but true isn't one of them. Alcoholic number one, Daryl, is drilling holes in the planks, most of them crooked or missing the nailers entirely. Alcoholic number two, Steve, is coming behind him, shooting the heads of the deck screws a quarter of an inch into the boards, the solution from the treated pine bubbling up in the holes.

Then one of the planks splits. "Goddamn it," Daryl says. "Goddamn it." He flings his hands up, swiping his baseball cap sideways. "That's enough, goddamn it. I need some lunch."

Junior lets off the circular saw. "It ain't even eleven o'clock."

"Horseshit it ain't." Daryl straightens his ball cap. "Besides, eleven o'clock means we been working for more'n an hour. I need a break."

"You been breaking. Every ten fucking minutes for beer and ciga-rettes."

"Bullshit." Daryl digs a beer out of the cooler. "Beer and a ciga-rette then." He sits down on the edge of the deck frame.

Steve looks up from his drill. "We breaking?"

"We're breaking." Daryl fishes his cigarettes out of his shirt pocket. "Fuck this slave driver. We ain't niggers. We're breaking for a goddamn cigarette."

Junior spits in the dirt and squats down on his heels beside the sawhorse. "Y'all won't never drown in sweat, will you?"

Daryl lifts his shirt and wipes his face, his hairless gut like an albino watermelon streaked with purple stretch marks. "Fuck you."

"Fuck you?"

"That's what I said."

"Let's not start this shit," Steve says.

Junior pulls his handkerchief out of his pocket very slowly and dabs at his bad eye with it. "Fuck you?" he says again.

"You hard of hearing?" Daryl asks him. "You treat us like we're a couple of niggers. You can't treat us however you want. Yeah, fuck you."

Junior stuffs his handkerchief in his pocket and starts to respond. But then a truck door slams closed out on the street. Junior looks over. "I'll be damned," he says.

"Who's that?" asks Steve.

Junior walks through his gate, out on the sidewalk. Patterson Wells stands leaning against the door of his truck. His left thumb is hooked in his belt, his right hand resting behind his hip, next to the butt of his not-very-well-concealed .45. He's compact and sunburnt, wearing a greasy Avrilla ball cap and a week or two of stubble. He looks older than Junior thought he was. Maybe forty-five, and a hard forty-five at that. One of those who's always short on sleep and lives mostly in his own head.

Junior stops a few feet back of him, and Patterson unhooks his thumb from his belt and slides a wad of cash out of his pocket. He tosses it in the dirt at Junior's feet. "What's that?" Junior asks, without looking at it.

"That's the money Henry owes you," Patterson says. "Two hundred dollars."

"You don't pay Henry's debts."

"I'm paying this one," Patterson says. "I don't want to see you down there no more."

"Whyn't you toss that gun in the dirt and we'll talk about it?" Junior says. "We'll discuss it right here."

"I ain't looking for trouble."

"Sure you ain't looking for trouble. Take that gun out and throw it on the ground right there," Junior says. "Then we'll talk about my old man."

"I ain't here to fight."

"No you ain't. You sure as hell ain't here to fight." Junior licks his lips. "You don't know a fucking thing. You got no idea who that old man is. There ain't a goddamn thing I could do to him that he don't deserve."

"That's his opinion, too," Patterson says. "I'm choosing to disagree."

"Horseshit. He's an old cunt. If I gave him half a chance he'd shoot me in the face. You think he's changed 'cause he got sober. He ain't changed."

"Goddamn," Darryl chortles behind Junior. "You talk like that about your own daddy, Junior?" He shakes his head at the very idea, a strand of saliva between his cigarette and his bottom lip waffling in the lean breeze.

Junior turns and leans down, scooping up a handful of rocks. "Get back to work," he says to Daryl.

"I'm almost done with my cigarette," Daryl says. "I done told you about treating me like a nigger."

Junior wings a rock sidehand at him, catching him right above his left eye.

Daryl jumps to his feet. "What the fuck?" His swollen face sets with a kind of alcoholic grandeur. The second rock catches him on the bridge of the nose. He sets his hands on his hips, eyeing Junior.

"Get back to work." Junior lets the rest of the rocks fall out of his hand.

"Fuck you."

Junior gives him a short left hook to the side of the head. Daryl jumps back to dodge a follow-up right and his ankle turns in the dirt with a knuckle pop. His leg crumbles inward under him and he falls back on his ass. "You son of a bitch." He pulls his ankle up into his lap, tears welling in his eyes.

Junior kicks him in the thigh. "You're fired, you sorry motherfucker."

"You're an asshole," Steve says. He starts gathering his tools into a cheap plastic toolbox.

"Get your ass back to work," says Junior.

"I ain't getting back to work," Steve says. "I'm done."

"You ain't getting no pay."

"Yeah. Fuck you and your pay." He bends down and takes Daryl by the elbow, helping him up. "You need to learn how to work with people," he says to Junior. They limp out of the yard.

Junior stands, staring at the ground and letting the adrenaline trickle off down his spine. It takes him a few minutes.

"You're hard on your friends," Patterson says.

Junior looks over as if just remembering he's there, all the anger run out of him. "You want to make some money?" he asks.

scope

It was curiosity that had convinced Patterson to take Junior up on his offer. When Patterson had said Henry's name, some small roughing had happened behind Junior's face. It was like watching stone fall away from a sculpture, the way he revealed himself, and Patterson wanted to see more of it. Not to hear Junior's story, Patterson knows enough to distrust stories. Just to see Junior operate a little. To see what he can of Henry in the way Junior moves.

So they work together quietly. Neither of them knows shit for carpentry, but it turns out to be a fine little deck. And when they drive the last screw Junior pulls two hundred dollars out of his pocket, the same two hundred dollars Patterson had tossed at his feet that morning, and passes it to him. "How'd you find me?" he asks.

"I ain't gonna answer that," Patterson says. The answer is easy enough, though. He'd had Emma look through Henry's loft while the old man was outside throwing up his hungover guts. And sure enough, Henry'd had Junior's address written down in a steno note-book by his phone.

"It don't matter," Junior says. "I'm getting cleaned up and going for a beer. If you wanna come, I'll buy you one."

They walk up the street to a little Mexican bar, a freestanding brick building next to a junkyard. One long room inside, with a few rickety booths and a clothes washer with a Post-it note on the door that reads "$57" at one end of the pitted wooden bar. There aren't many other patrons. A pair of dark-skinned girls, exactly the kind of women Patterson doesn't have any need to be looking at anymore. Lean bodies, eyes pleading boredom with everything Denver has to offer. They're with two young men wearing tank top undershirts, khaki shorts, and tennis shoes, who're talking to the bartender in Spanish. The bartender's older and bigger, probably Junior's age, dressed up in a Western shirt and black crocodile belly boots, a small glass of tequila in front of him.

Junior slides into the first booth and fingers a cigarette out of his pack. "Where you from, Patterson?" he asks.

"Right here," Patterson answers, taking the other side of the booth, which squeals and shudders in protest.

"Right here, meaning North Denver?"

"Right here, meaning Denver. East Colfax."

"Do you smoke?"

Patterson pulls out his cigarettes and holds them up.

"Good man." Junior points at Patterson with his cigarette. "Do you know about the Sand Creek massacre?"

"I've read about it."

"Did you know that afterward, Chivington and his boys rode through Denver with women's cunts stretched over their saddle bows and pinned across their hats? Carrying Indian kid's hearts and fetuses on sticks."

"I've read that, too," Patterson says.

"Friend of mine told me about it," Junior says. "Vicente. All he does is read about shit like that." He lights his cigarette. "The people of Denver threw them a ticker-tape parade, did you know that?"

"Yep," Patterson says.

Junior nods. "That ain't what gets me, though. The cunts on a stick and the ticker-tape parade, that ain't it."

"It's enough for me."

"The thing that gets me is that now you can't even smoke a fucking cigarette in a bar. Back then you could walk down the street with a woman's cunt on a stick, and now you get treated like a pedophile for smoking a cigarette." He snorts in disgust.

Patterson doesn't point out that they're both smoking cigarettes in the bar right there. Instead he looks over at the girls, can't help it, and catches them looking right back at him. Or looking at Junior, anyway. And he can't blame them. Junior's showered and shaved, putting on fresh jeans and a Rockmount shirt and his eye patch, and he has all of Henry's hard and boyish good looks on display. The little light that's managed to struggle through the unwashed front window seems to hover around him, wavering when he moves to draw on his cigarette or kick his boots up on the bar chair across from him. Patterson knows just enough about cowboy boots to know that they're handcrafted hornbacks, and that he's owned cars that cost less.

"You gonna lecture me about Henry?" Junior asks.

Patterson pulls his attention away from the girls. By force. They've set a hole blossoming open in his chest that he knows he doesn't have any hope of filling. "I can't let you come up there and kick the shit out of him whenever you feel like it."

"You can't let me," Junior says scornfully. "He's lucky I didn't use a tire jack, the motherfucker. You wanna know what he said that set me off?"

Patterson shakes his head. "Not even a little."

"All right," Junior says. "Tell you what. As long as he doesn't repeat it, I won't whip his ass again."

"How's about this," Patterson says. "How's about the next time you get the urge to start beating on him, you give me a call? How's about we have a drink and talk it over."

Junior looks at him. "I'll do my best," he says.

They stop talking for a minute. The girls aren't even trying to hide their interest in Junior from their boyfriends anymore. One of them, the longer and prettier of the two, says something to the other, and they both smile. Their boyfriends are hunched on their elbows at the bar now, talking low to the bartender. The first thought that goes through Patterson's head is that he's way too old for this shit. The second is that he wouldn't leave the bar now if you put a screwdriver to his temple.

"That one there, she's something," Junior says.

"The other one, too," Patterson says. "Which one were you talking about?"

"I don't suppose it matters."

"I don't suppose it does," Patterson says. Then, "Do you know what scope lock means?"

"Go ahead," Junior says.

"It's a military term."

"I wouldn't have guessed you for the military."

"I wasn't," Patterson says. "I read it somewhere."

"You read a lot," Junior says. "So it's a secondhand military term?"

"That's right."

It could be the light, but it looks an awful lot like Junior winks at one of the girls. Though with the eye patch, he could have just been blinking.

"So what's it mean?" Junior asks.

"It means when somebody only gets their information from one source, and it starts to affect their thinking."

"Like Henry and that fucking radio show he listens to? Brother Joe?"

"Yeah," Patterson says. "And other things."

Junior laughs out loud at that. "Go fuck yourself." He draws a vial of cocaine out of his pocket and cuts two lines on the booth's tabletop with his pocketknife. The bartender looks over at them and looks away. Junior snorts one of the lines and passes Patterson the straw. Patterson hesitates. "Go ahead," Junior says. "They ain't going to call the cops. Ain't one of them legal."

Patterson takes the straw and snorts the other line while Junior cuts more. When he's done there are twelve, each of which would kill a large child outright and drown most adults in postnasal drip. "I got enough for everybody," Junior calls to the girls. The long one licks her lips and all the breath goes out of Patterson. But she doesn't approach. "Calm down, Patterson," Junior says. "We're just fishing." His good eye glitters like that of a child arsonist.

I probably should shoot him right here, Patterson thinks. Instead he does another line.

The main problem with cocaine is that you never really have enough of it. Even on a binge, you've usually got just enough to keep yourself in nosebleeds and self-hatred. But Junior cuts lines like other people serve beers, and inside of a half hour he and Patterson are falling-out-of-the-booth high. And Junior's pitching the girls, calling to them every ten minutes or so that he has more cocaine back at his house, a whole lot more, and plenty of beer. It isn't the kind of offer that'd work on every girl, probably. Just every girl Patterson's ever known. Then Junior winks at Patterson across the booth. "Watch the coke," he says. And he stands wobbling out of his chair and saunters down the bar, disappearing into the restroom hallway at the back of the bar.

To their credit, the Mexican boys wait nearly thirty seconds before following him.

Patterson picks up the vial of cocaine and slips it in his pocket. The bartender moves out from behind the bar, meeting him in front of the hallway. "They're fine," he says. "There is no trouble here." He's holding a little Raven .25 automatic in his right hand.

"Sure," Patterson says. "I just need to take a piss." There's a loud thump from the direction of the bathroom. Then a strangled high sound, like a pig's squeal, that cuts off in the middle.

"Piss in the alley," the bartender says, grinning. "Your friend is fine."

Patterson turns and walks back toward the front door, ignoring the other sounds coming from the bathroom. Just thuds now, like somebody stomping on a pumpkin. The girls sit in the booth, ramrod straight, their eyes craterous, shell-shocked.

But Patterson had one of those little Raven .25s in his younger days. Bought it for fifty bucks at an Ohio flea market. He got drunk the night he bought it and fired off an entire magazine at a tree that couldn't have been seven feet in front of him, and managed to miss with every shot. When Patterson's put four paces between himself and the bartender, he swings around, pulling out his .45, and puts his front sight right on the man's chest.

"You pussy," the bartender says, but he doesn't raise the .25. Patterson figures he's probably shot it once or twice himself. "You are a fucking pussy."

"Put it down and turn around," Patterson says.

"You pussy," the bartender says again. But he places the pistol on the bar and turns around.

Patterson grabs him by his thin black hair and shoves him down the hallway, through the men's room door.

It's over. Junior's washing his hands in the sink. One of the boys' legs are sticking out from the stall and the other is slumped against the wall, staring senseless through bloodred eyeballs, the capillaries exploded. The bartender's breath hisses out between his teeth.

Junior shakes water off his hands. "I was wondering if you were going to show," he says to Patterson. Then he takes the bartender by the back of the neck, like you might take a friend to draw him in to tell him something. Patterson lets go of the bartender and steps back.

"You're a pussy, too," the bartender says into Junior's ear.

Junior shoots a rabbit punch into his gut, and when the bartender tries to hustle back to get some boxing room, Patterson grabs him by the cheek and slams his head into the wall. Patterson doesn't like having guns pointed at him, and doesn't particularly give a shit for the reason. The bartender doesn't even try to resist after that, and Junior makes short work of him. First fists, then boots.

"Now I got to wash my hands again," Junior says when he's done.

Justin

I didn't keep a gun around the house when we had you. They make your mom nervous, for one thing. For another, there didn't seem a whole lot of need when I was working Questa and Taos. I looked forward to teaching you how to shoot, though. I don't hunt much, but I like skeet shooting. I figured that sooner or later I'd buy a little .410 single shot for your own. I had it in my mind. Just like teaching you how to throw a baseball. Or fishing. All of those father-and-son moments you see on television. But shooting was one of those many things I didn't get around to when you were alive. It seems like my memory's nothing but a series of holes where those moments should be. Moments I spent drinking beer, sitting on the front porch. Moments I spent wondering how the hell I ended up settled down in Questa, New Mexico.

It was only after you died that I started carrying a gun full-time. I was in Louisiana, just after Hurricane Katrina. I'd never carried one up until then, even when I was working with the worst crews. Most of the men I was with aren't exactly opposed to violence. That comes with the job. Hell, when you're young, it's part of the attraction. When you still give a shit about things like whether you can hold your own in a fight, you're more than happy to work with those kind of men.

It's a job that attracts that kind, I guess. The kind of men who get shaken out of normal life and collected at the bottom. I ain't saying everybody, but I doubt there's any occupation with a greater percentage of convicts, drunks, and addicts. It's just the way it is. Even so, they never scared me enough I felt like I needed a gun. A good clip knife was fine.

Besides which, almost all the danger we faced came from our work. Especially since the men I worked with didn't exactly hold safety as their highest priority. I know I didn't when I was younger. I worked an entire season once dropping LSD every morning, and I don't know anybody who works strictly sober. Men fall out of trees, men amputate themselves, and when there ain't easy access to medical help, men bleed out. When that happens, there's not a whole lot to do but watch them die while the foreman tries to call whoever the hell he's supposed to. A gun's not of much use in that situation.

But Louisiana after Katrina, that was different. Where we were camped, you could hear gunfire most hours of the night or day, and we weren't even close to the worst of it. We just tried to keep our heads down, work on clearing the lines of debris, and let everything else take care of itself. But still, we heard stories about what was going down. People being gunned down by vigilantes and rogue cops. Whole blocks tagged "Dead Body Inside," nobody even bothering to remove them. Refugees from the city being turned away at gunpoint from higher ground.

We didn't belong there. Everybody knew we didn't belong there. And we were working equipment worth hundreds of thousands of dollars, all of which was exactly what every person there needed. Most things lose their value after a hurricane, but bucket trucks and chain saws don't, not for anybody who's got a house buried under rubble. We were targets and there wasn't one of us who didn't know it.

And then there were the bigger stories. Blackwater mercenaries cleaning out the most desirable New Orleans real estate. Developers buying up the newly vacated land, planning condos, already rebuilding New Orleans as a cheap theme park of itself. Corporations moving in to take over everything they could get their hands on, right down to the schools and hospitals. And the big story, the one everybody believed. That the Lower Ninth Ward levees had been deliberately breached, smashed by a barge in order to save the French Quarter. I didn't meet a single person who lived near the levees who didn't tell me that story.

It was hearing those stories that made me realize I wanted something besides a pocketknife to protect myself. It was not having any idea what was actually going on. So I bought a 1911 from a street kid I found walking a wheelbarrow of looted goods past our bucket truck in Jefferson Parish. He told me it was junk, that it'd jam up every time after the first round, so I only had to give him a hundred dollars for it.

The thing is, I knew exactly what was wrong with the gun the minute that street kid told me the problem. My father, your grandfather, he carried one of those every day of his life. He was a Vietnam veteran and he didn't go anywhere without his service issue .45 Colt 1911A1. One of the many gifts given him by the Vietnam War was that he had more conspiracy theories than Brother Joe, and all his theories made him feel a hell of a lot better armed.

So I sat down in the street right there, took the extractor out of the slide, and tensioned it with my thumbs. It's run like a top ever since, and when I got back to Colorado that summer, I applied for my concealed-carry permit. It's good in most states, and now I've got just one rule. I won't work anywhere I can't carry. That's my only rule.

jobs

Junior's driving. He's been driving all day. When he doesn't have any runs to make for Vicente, he ends up spending most of every day driving anyway. Knowing every minute of it that he should be with Casey.

Junior's mother was a good mother. Broken and sad from having married a piece of shit, but a good mother. It was that goodness that made Junior feel guilty most of the time. He knew what Henry was, and even from a young age, he knew that he and Henry were partners in it, in making his mother cry. He knew because he could do it just as easy as Henry could. And did so, without even trying.

When Junior first saw Casey, was handed her at the hospital, that was one thing he knew he wasn't going to do to her. He wasn't going to put that kind of guilt in her. That's what he thought back then, that children were some kind of little machines that ran on the guilt adults pumped into them. Now he knows better. Now he knows it's exactly the other way around.

He drives north, Seventieth to Pecos, toward the heart of Denver, Federal Boulevard. The Rustic Ranch Mobile Home Park, Pyro Fireworks. Homeless bagsippers and lowrider pimps. Then back toward the empty backroads of unincorporated Adams County and Commerce City, watching the evening get suffocated by the fumes of the oil refinery.

From the street, Junior can see Jenny's bedroom light burning behind the dirty box fan in her window. He spins the car around, parks out in front of her house. Slips a little in his cowboy boots as he steps out of the car. It's been a long day of beer drinking and driving. When he gets up to her house, she's sitting on the front stoop, smoking a cigarette. "I was betting you'd stop by tonight," she says. "I still got that joint."

"Light it," he says. "I need something, and I can't drink no more beer."

"That was your excuse last time," she says. "Too much beer."

"Are you gonna light the joint?"

She pulls it out of her pack of cigarettes and sparks it. "My interview went real good, thanks for asking." She exhales a stream of smoke up toward the streetlights, passes it to him. The night air has cleared out the big stink and the heat, leaving the neighborhood almost as cool and fresh as the San Luis Valley. "They already called me back for a second."

Junior hits the joint and passes it back to her. "I've got plenty of money," he says, exhaling. "May not have much else, but I got plenty of money."

"That's not the point," she says. "Casey and I can't live here forever."

"So move," Junior says. "You don't need a fucking job to move."

She pauses for a drag. "You know what I saw the other day? I saw

a pit bull walking down the street, loose. No owner, nobody around."
She pushes the joint toward him, he waves it off.

"You saw a loose dog," he says. "That's what started all this?"

"Casey can't play outside. Can't play in the yard, even when the
air's good. And I wouldn't even think about letting one of her friends
visit. I'd die first."

Junior looks around the yard. A few islands of dry grass in a sea
of dust, a rubbery black patch where the last tenant parked his car on
blocks. "So move," he says. "Start looking for a place right now. I got
plenty of money."

"Yeah," she says. "But I want a job." She finishes the joint, the
moon wandering in and out of the night clouds. "What's on your
mind?" she asks. "Something's wrong."

He pulls his handkerchief out of his pocket with more flourish
than he means to, puts it to his eye. "Hell if I know."

"Do you ever get worried, Junior? How you never seem to know
what's wrong with you?"

He looks at her. "I don't know."

"I do," she says. "I know what's wrong with you."

"Well. Whyn't you tell me then?"

"You shouldn't be doing what you're doing. It's hurting you."

"Driving?"

"Yes, driving."

"What the hell else would I do? I sure as fuck ain't going back to
day labor."

"It's a question," she says. "It's a question for you to answer. All I
know is that when I get a job, you will have time to answer it."

"Shit," Junior says.

"You're scared of the idea, aren't you?" Her eyes glitter, girlishly
cruel, and she chews on her thumbnail.

Junior stands. "I'm leaving. I ain't got time for this shit."

The girlish twinkle disappears from her eyes. They're mother now. "I mean it, Junior. You need to find something else to do."

"There ain't nothing," Junior says, sitting again.

The moonlight washes some of the exhaustion clean from her face and she looks almost as young as she actually is. She rests her head on his shoulder. "We've got to get out of here," she says, her voice bruised soft with exhaustion and marijuana. "I'm going to get this job and we're gonna get the hell out of here."

spider goats

It takes Patterson a few days to get over his trip to Denver. He's too old for cocaine, and far too old for bar fights. But finally he makes the drive over to Henry's that he knows he needs to make.

The old man's poking around for something inside his Wild Mustang Mesa truck, parked up by the stables. He backs out of the driver's door holding his computer, a chunky piece of hardware encased in black, military-grade polymer. "Hello, Patterson," he says. His face is healing, the old skin flaking off and the new coming in pink and tender.

"Hello, Henry," Patterson says, stepping out of his truck. "That's a hell of a computer."

"It's indestructible," Henry says. "They bought it for the horses. We track them now using wireless sensors. We can even tell if they're being mounted."

"Mounted?"

"To make sure they're breeding."

"Damn," Patterson says, impressed.

Henry looks at Patterson for a minute, like he's deciding whether or not to tell him something. Then he makes up his mind. "Spider goats," he says.

"Say what?"

Henry sets the computer on the hood of his truck and opens it. "I just heard about 'em on the radio. Brother Joe says they're goats that spin silk like spiders. Only instead of being regular spider silk it's stronger than Kevlar. The feds are going to start making body armor out of it."

Patterson doesn't say anything.

"There ain't no need for that shit," Henry says. "I can see what you're thinking."

"I'm thinking the altitude is affecting your brain," Patterson says.

Henry pushes a button on the computer. It clunks to life and he punches a few buttons more. Then he swivels the computer screen around so Patterson can see it. "See?"

Patterson squints at the screen. "Looks like a regular goat."

"Well, it ain't," Henry says. "It's a spider goat." He turns the screen back around and shuts the computer.

"I'd have thought it'd look like a spider," Patterson says.

"I don't know why I show you anything," Henry says. He shoves the computer back in the truck. "What do you want?"

"I've been meaning to tell you that I went up to Denver."

Henry's face doesn't exactly change expression, but every line in it deepens, threatening to fissure completely. "Why'd you do that?"

"To talk to Junior."

Henry leans against his truck. "Why?"

"You know why."

"At least he didn't kill you," he says.

"I helped him put a deck on his house. And then we got drunk."

"Well. That should teach him."

"We came to an agreement," Patterson says. "He's going to call me if he gets it in his head to see you. He's going to stop by my place first and we'll talk it over."

"You can't trust him." Henry shakes his head. "I was hard on him, but it wasn't all me. You never could trust him."

"I can trust him. I'm not sure I ever want to get drunk with him again, but I can trust him to keep his word."

Henry smoothes his beard with his hand, a smile toying around with his mouth. "Bit off more'n you could chew?"

Patterson shakes his head. "I'm lucky to be alive."

Henry laughs. "He's a wild one, that's for sure."

"I heard you were, too."

"I was," Henry says. "Someday I'll have to tell you the whole story."

"That's all right."

"Thanks for keeping me informed, anyway." Henry claps him on the shoulder. "Now, I got something to show you. Follow me." He picks up his crutches and leads Patterson around back of his cabin. "That's what you need." He points with his cane at a series of solar panels mounted on a PVC frame on the roof. "There ain't nothing to it. A little PVC, a few panels, golf batteries, a charge controller, and an AC to DC inverter. It's a sweet little setup, and it won't cost you more than a few hundred bucks."

Patterson squints up at the panels, the sun reflecting off them in a hard, black-yellow burst. "You build it yourself?"

"I paid a Mexican boy off our crew to do most of the actual work. Been meaning to show it to you."

A gust of wind throws dust across the mesa. Patterson lifts his Avrilla ball cap from his head and uses it to shield the side of his face from it, looking up at the solar panel. Then he reseats his cap on his head. "Just the laptop?"

"A little refrigerator, too. And I've got plenty left over for a radio and a lamp at night. Even got a little television with a DVD player if I want it. More than that, I don't need. We could set you up in a weekend."

"Living off the grid," Patterson says.

"Living off the grid," Henry repeats. "You know what you ought to do?"

"Bet you're gonna tell me."

"You ought to let your wife add your name to that lawsuit. Get you enough money you can stay here full-time."

"She's not my wife anymore." Then, "And how the hell do you know anything about it?"

"She came up looking for you while you were in Denver. I was happening by your cabin to show you the solar setup. We talked."

Patterson sticks his thumbs in his pockets and eyes the hardware. Then he looks away. Up ahead, a golden eagle playing across the washed-out sky. Here disappearing in a flash of sun, there emerging against a strip of thin cloud. "It's complicated."

"It's always complicated," Henry says. His face crowds with whatever he's thinking. Then he says it. "Believe me, Patterson, I know how much you miss your son. But it's about time. And that gal thinks the world of you."

Patterson does what he can to throttle his pulse and just nods. "What would you suggest I do for work?"

"I could talk to Paulson. You could clear brush for home pads and keep the roads clear."

"It's complicated," Patterson says again, lamely. The eagle screams. It dives fifty or sixty feet and levels off, soaring out of sight.

smaller

They sit in the garage, eating pizza and drinking beer out of brown bottles, the last yellow light of day striking through the bay doors and dust-washed windows. Junior's never known two men as different as these two. Vicente small and wiry and bespectacled, his hair cropped close on his skull, erratic in speech and movement. Eduardo built more like a small mountain, heavily tattooed, with long black hair and the demeanor of a warrior king out of a children's book. They sit shoulder to shoulder together, and it occurs to Junior that he's never known them to have any friends other than him. That they live almost entirely in isolation, moving together with the familiarity of old dogs.

"You still thinking about getting out of the speed business?" Junior asks.

"I'm still thinking about it," Vicente says. He looks at Junior, his eyes blinking rapidly. "I am sick of hearing about methamphetamines.

All this you see on television, that methamphetamines are some new scourge. There's nothing new."

"I don't watch television," Junior says.

"That is wise." Vicente nods. "It's better to play chess. Or even do what you do, drink beer and snort cocaine. Television will make you stupid. The things they say about methamphetamines, this is evidence."

"Go ahead," Junior says.

"This drug that is now the worst drug ever invented, do you know where it came from? I will tell you. It was invented as a diet drug, prescribed to housewives to control their weight. And now everyone is supposed to be scared of it. Why do you think that is?"

"No idea," Junior says.

"They want everyone in prison, that's why. Everyone they can't make a use for. There are no new drugs, so they repackage old drugs. The worst drug ever, they say. They invented crack from cocaine to lock away the niggers, now they're locking you gringos away over diet pills."

"I never asked where you get it from, the meth," Junior says. "I just pick it up. I know I ain't the only driver, can't be, don't care. And as to the rest of your operation, it don't mean shit to me."

"True," Vicente says. "You never ask anything. That is one of the things I like about you."

Junior removes his eye patch and presses the heel of his hand against the bad eye. His hand comes away wet and he wipes it on his jeans. Then he thinks another minute before he asks what he knows he's going to ask. "Is it La Familia?"

Vicente nods. "That's who produces it, yes. Those are the people I was speaking of the other day."

"Do you have any of those books? The ones they carry around with their sayings."

"No," Vicente says. "The books are written by their leader. He is known as El Más Loco."

"El Más Loco?" Junior repeats.

"That's right," Vicente says.

"Does that mean the most crazy one?"

"That's what it means. They are not subtle, this family."

"Just a moment," Eduardo says. He stands and walks back through the cars and parts and toolboxes, disappearing for a minute, and then returning with a grease-stained paperback in his hand. "Here." He hands the book to Junior.

Junior turns it over in his hand. "*Brave of Heart*," he reads. "Like the movie?"

"No." Eduardo shakes his head. "This is about the heart you share with God. The heart that must be brave to be shared."

"What is it?" Vicente asks.

"It's the book they get their sayings from," Eduardo says.

"Is that true?" Vicente asks. "Who wrote it?"

"A preacher in Colorado Springs." Eduardo stuffs most of a slice of pizza in his mouth and swallows it in a lump. "A gringo who climbs mountains. They carry the book of sayings, but they must read this one before they are allowed to be members of La Familia."

"The preacher lives in Colorado Springs?" Vicente asks.

"It's globalization," Eduardo says, nodding. "The world gets smaller every day."

"Read something from it," Vicente says to Junior.

Junior opens a page and reads at random. "Most Christians live by archaic laws," he reads. "They live Jeremiah 17:9, 'The heart is deceitful above all things and beyond cure,' and give their hearts away to those that are not worthy of it. They waste their hearts on television and newspapers, they squander it in kitchenettes and malls. The only questions that matter are buried in your heart, and it is a heart worthy of God. Brave, wild, bloody, and most of all free. And, yes, all of our hearts have been broken, but you must trust Him to heal them."

"Gibberish," says Vicente. "Craziness."

"You can keep it," Eduardo says to Junior.

"You can borrow it," Vicente corrects. "I will read it when you're done."

"All right," Junior says.

Vicente removes his glasses and wipes them on his shirt. He still looks a little rattled, but when he returns his glasses to his face, he is recovered. "Now I have a question for you," he says.

"Shoot."

"Do you know a man named Patterson Wells?"

"Yeah, I know him," Junior says, reading the book's back matter.

"There is a man looking for him."

Junior looks up from the book. "What man?"

"I don't know," Vicente says. "His name is Chase. He has been all over Denver, giving out his phone number. He claims Patterson Wells has stolen crystal meth from him, a large amount. He is offering a thousand-dollar reward to anyone who will tell him where Patterson Wells lives."

Junior holds the book against his leg. "Did you get his phone number?"

mousegun

The Hi-U Inn sits on a nearly dead highway running out of Commerce City, an industrial suburb north of Denver. It's a jumble of tacked-up felt paper and plywood, with a dilapidated sign in the shape of a cowboy waving motorists off the road and into the parking lot. Junior parks by a small common area under a sagging second-story porch. Dogshit-stained outdoor carpeting, a couple of plastic garden chairs, a deck table with a crooked sun umbrella.

The door to one of the units whips open. "Goddamn, you're a speedy motherfucker," Chase says. He's wired, tweaking, addict scrawny. "You got here quick."

Junior slides his keys into his pocket. "Can I come in?" he asks.

"Yeah. Hell, yeah." Chase moves out of the way. "You want a beer or something?"

Junior steps into the narrow kitchenette. It reeks of iodine and burning plastic.

"Sit. Sit down." Chase motions to a cigarette-pocked Formica table. "I was thinking about having some ramen." He sticks the fingers of his right hand into his left armpit and digs furiously. "You want some?"

"I'm all right." Junior takes a seat.

"I was just thinking about it. I hadn't started making it or anything."

"Sit down," Junior says. "You're making me nervous."

"Yeah, I can do that." Chase pulls out a chair across from Junior and sits in it. Fidgeting with the scabs on his hands.

"How do you know Patterson Wells?" Junior asks.

"We used to work together," Chase says.

"You two worked together?"

"I wasn't always like I am," Chase says. "I've had a lot of shit go wrong in my life."

"I ain't judging you, partner."

"Good." His chin quivers. "He fucked me up. It tears me up, but he did."

"What'd he do?"

"He took my wife. He stole from me, too. But he took my wife, that's the main thing."

"You got a picture?" Junior asks.

Chase lifts a duffel bag off the floor. He roots around for a minute and comes up with a crumpled photograph. He tries to smooth it out on his thigh, fails, and hands it to Junior, still crumpled. Then reaches for it as if to try to smooth it out again, but Junior is already holding it. "She's a good-looking woman," Junior says.

Chase's face reddens sharply and his top lip skins back over his canines. "I'll kill him when I find him," he hisses. "I mean it, too."

"She's got to be at least ten years younger'n you," Junior says.

"Eight," says Chase. "Maybe nine."

"She a tweaker, too?"

"You said you wasn't going to judge me," Chase whines. His chin starts bobbing up and down. At first Junior thinks it means he's going to start crying. Then the bobbing increases, and takes on a weird elliptical motion. "That's what you said."

"Will you hold your fucking head still?" Junior says. Then, "Is she?"

"She does a little bit. Weekends and shit. She's a businesswoman." Chase's brow furrows in concentration and his hands still. He holds them on his thighs. His head keeps moving, though.

"So not like you," Junior says. "Not a complete fucking burnout."

"What are you getting at?" Chase says. "What are you trying to say?"

"I'm trying to figure out what a girl like that would be doing with an ugly little tweaker like you," Junior says. "I'd have thought the question was obvious."

"Fuck you," Chase says. His right hand trembles again. He sticks it in between his legs. Then he concentrates again, and even his head stills. But his left foot shoots out, kicking into the table. "Do you know where he is or not? I don't need this shit."

"If he ain't fucking her, somebody is," Junior says. "Hell, if I find her, I'll probably take a run at her." He tosses the photograph on the table. "I'd give this one up, partner. There was no chance in hell she was going to stay with you once the crank ran out."

Chase jumps to his feet, his left hand thrusting in his pocket. Junior grabs his forearm and closes his other hand on Chase's throat, driving his thumb up under Chase's jawbone. Chase rasps for breath and pisses himself. A little .380 mousegun drops on the floor. "There it is," Junior says. "That's what we're looking for."

pictures

Patterson can't stop thinking about Laney. Just like, he's pretty sure, Henry meant him to. He starts out furious that Laney came up and wormed her way into his life, and then he just can't stop thinking about her. And about her lawsuit. About what she said. Their duty to other children, to other parents. To himself. That he needs some kind of closure. It's the kind of talk that sends him spinning straight off the road. He doesn't have the kind of grip on the wheel necessary for duties anymore, and talk about closure is enough to drive him straight into a stump.

This morning, he knows he just needs to stop thinking about it. He needs to sit awhile in the cool recesses of a bar. Sit for a long while, thinking about nothing. A baseball game, maybe. There's nothing that can still clear out his head like a baseball game.

So he loads up and drives down south into the flat scrubland of New Mexico. Through Questa, a patch of ad hoc restaurants and bars that look like they were designed by a scatterbrained meth head with no depth perception, into the coyote fences and adobe houses of Taos, and to a sports bar in a low-slung shopping center right before the southern limit of the town.

It's exactly as cool and dark as he wants. Reeking of perfume and lager, the lights dialed down to a low blue. And, sure enough, the large-screen television is tuned into a baseball game. But just when the bartender is pouring his first drink, his cell phone rings.

"Are you in town?" Laney asks.

"How did you know that?" Patterson says. "How in the hell'd you know that?"

"You drove through downtown. Three people called, one person emailed, and two more texted. You know how it is."

"Yeah. I should have gone to Alamosa."

"I thought if you were in town I'd meet you. I have something I want to give you."

"I'm at the sports bar," Patterson says, and hangs up. And then he wonders why he hadn't gone to Alamosa, which has just as many bars as Taos. But he knows the answer, knew it already.

Not five minutes later, she slings her purse down on the bar. She's wearing a banker's blouse that Patterson already knows he's going to spend most of their time together trying not to peek down. "Where's the boy?" he asks.

"He's in day care. I'm working." She turns to the bartender. "Vodka and tonic." Then, when he scampers off to fetch it for her, she bends to Patterson and kisses him on the cheek. Her drink comes, and she sips it through the cocktail straw. "I've got some pictures you haven't seen," she says. "That's what I wanted to give you."

The idiot in the mirror in front of Patterson looks like he might disintegrate. "I don't need them," Patterson says. He rearranges the idiot's face, telling him that he better pull his shit together. Then he asks, "What are they of?"

"Camping on the Rio Grande Gorge. They were in one of those little disposable cameras you used to buy. I found it in the closet." She unzips her purse and pulls out a packet of photographs. "You want to see them?"

Patterson shakes his head, his eyes locked on the baseball game. Not in front of her.

She slides the packet across the bar to him. "These are copies. You can take them with you."

He takes a drink of his beer.

"Poor Patterson," she says. "Everything's still that hard for you, isn't it?"

He doesn't answer. He knows what she's up to. And she knows that he knows what she's up to. They were married too long.

She puts her hand on his arm and squeezes. "I'm sorry."

"How's about you take the rest of the day off work?" he says. "The rest of the week, maybe. How's about we get a couple of bottles of bourbon and a hotel room. Hole up for a few days. Just the two of us."

"There is no two of us," she says, her hand still on his arm. "There's no two of anybody if you're one of them. I had to learn that the hard way."

Patterson doesn't bother arguing with her.

She lets go of his arm and sips her drink. "Do you still write to him?"

"All the time," he answers without hesitation. Then he adds, "Sort of."

"Sort of, meaning you don't write to him all the time?"

"Sort of, meaning I'm not sure it's him I'm writing to anymore."

"I had the same problem," she says. "It's why I stopped. I was just writing down things that happened to me."

"I'm talking about my life," he says. "But I'm not sure who I'm talking to."

"Part of me wishes I hadn't stopped," she says. "I didn't understand it until I stopped."

"Understand what?"

"That the conversation had two sides. That his answer was in my trying to see everything I was doing through his eyes. But there are things now that I don't think it would be fair to share with him."

"He wouldn't care. I write shit all the time that no kid could understand."

"That's fine for you. He's still the only thing in your life. That's why you live up there on your mesa punishing yourself." She smiles at him. "I need to get back to work."

"That's a no to the hotel room?"

"I'm too old to survive a hotel room with you," she says.

"And here I've been feeling like I'm about the safest thing in my life," he says.

She taps the packet of pictures and stands. "Then you probably need to change company," she says.

Justin

I first met your mother in that sports bar. I don't know if I ever told you that, but I did. I never meant to meet anyone like her, either. I didn't have any interest in a wife. I know I haven't told you that, and probably shouldn't, but it's true. The truth is I was plenty happy with things just the way they were.

With Avrilla, I made what I thought was big money, didn't have any expenses but getting drunk, and traveled all over the country on their dime. Eighteen years old and I was walking the French Quarter in New Orleans, working my way through every bar on Rush Street in Chicago. Hitting the peep shows in North Beach, keeping company with some of the toughest men on the planet. It was a party. A party interrupted by backbreaking labor, the kind that you're lucky to survive, but a party. Settling down wasn't on my mind at all.

But then I was heading through Taos after a season of clearing power lines in Georgia, and I stopped for the night at the Super 8 next door to that sports bar. And when I walked over later, there she was, playing pool with two of her girlfriends. I had a couple of drinks at the bar and one of her friends asked me to join in on a game so's they could play doubles. So I did. Standing back against the wall most of the time, watching them play. Watching her.

She was something else, your mother. Enough younger'n me that it hurt a little to look at. Brown eyes that tended black when she was excited or pissed off. A perfect little mouth made to be bemused. I had a pretty good line of shit at the time and I ran it on her. She didn't mind so much that I didn't spend the night at her house instead of the motel.

After that I passed through Taos as often as I could. And when Laney found out she was pregnant with you, I quit Avrilla and got a job on a local landscaping crew, moving in with her. We had all the usual fights new parents have when you were born, but it was easier on us than it is on a lot of people. We were pretty good at going without sleep, if nothing else. We'd had plenty of hangovers by way of practice. And then you were gone, and we had no way of working through that.

I still don't.

It started as a rash on your leg. It was a Saturday morning, and the house was already steaming, startlingly hot for as early summer as it was. We didn't have air-conditioning and I was cooking break-fast with the windows open, trying to get us all fed before the heat came on hard. That's when Laney brought you in and showed it to me. You were a little man in Aquaman underwear. Your brown hair streaked your head, sweat beading at your temples. I told her there was nothing to worry about, that you'd be just fine as soon as we got some food in you.

But you wouldn't eat. And then you wouldn't talk. And then your temperature spiked, and your green eyes went flat. We drove you straight to Dr. Court's office, but he barely examined you. He glanced at your leg, cracked a couple of jokes, and told us it was heat rash, that you had heat exhaustion.

So we stopped by Walmart on the way home for an air conditioner. But it was less than an hour after I got it installed in your bedroom that you started having trouble breathing. And it was cardiac arrest by the time we got you to the hospital.

You never came out of the coma. You lasted two weeks. I was in the bathroom at the hospital when you died, and when I was stopped in the hallway on the way back, I didn't believe them. Not until I saw you. I had no way of knowing how to conceive of a world without you. I guess I still don't. It's like there's a notch that's been taken out of me, and I'm walking around just waiting to collapse in on myself.

When Dr. Court told you something you believed it. It was the kind of doctor he was. Because he wore being a doctor well. There are things you have to take on faith, because you don't know enough to even ask the right questions. And it's easy to take a man on faith if he's always joking with you like there's nothing he can't control. I used to say that anybody who argued with their doctor was an idiot. They don't tell me how to climb a tree with a chain saw in hand, I don't tell them how to do what they're paid to do. Now I don't pass one on the street without wanting to cut their face for pretending they know anything.

And I'll admit this, I'd been working sixteen-hour days, and I wanted an air conditioner. I'd been after your mother to buy one for weeks, but she kept saying we didn't have the money. I wanted Dr. Court to be right so I could spend the day with you in your room, in the cool air. So I trusted him on that, too.

jogging

Patterson pulls off the side of the road outside of Questa and flips through the pictures. The fucking pictures. There are only six of them, and he doubts he could describe them even a minute after looking at them. Except for his son. In particular, one of the boy's back as he stands staring across the Rio Grande Gorge, too near the edge. His brown hair is ruffled birdlike from the sleeping bag and, as young as he is, his shoulders are broad and square.

When he's done looking at them Patterson has to smoke a cigarette before he can drive again. And it takes all the self-control he has not to put it out on the back of his hand.

Then his cell phone rings. He answers it quick. Figuring he can make it back to Taos and Laney inside of fifteen minutes. Figuring where he can buy a bottle of bourbon on the way. Figuring he needs that bourbon and hotel room like a white woman in a John Wayne movie needs a last bullet.

"You jogging?" Junior asks.

"Jogging?" Patterson says.

"You're breathing hard, like you're either jogging or fucking," Junior says. "Jogging seemed likelier."

"I was driving."

"Driving. Well, good. You got a drive ahead of you."

"I do?"

"To Denver," he says. "I got something I need to show you."

Patterson doesn't have to think about it for long. Anything sounds better than sitting on his front porch. Whereas he started the spring planning his day around watching the sun set over the Blanca Massif, now he finds himself staring it down.

Patterson hadn't expected to see Junior again anytime soon. As a matter of fact, he'd meant to make that a rule. There are many things a man of Patterson's age shouldn't be doing, and pulling guns on Mexicans in their own bars is probably at the top of that list. But sometimes events conspire against you. And after seeing those fucking pictures he figures he's up for any trouble Junior can get them into.

He's wrong.

Junior's sitting on his couch with his cowboy boots kicked up on the coffee table, holding a remote control. When Patterson walks in through the screen door, he can't tell at first what the remote control is for. But then he follows Junior's eyes to the television mounted on the wall. It's the size of a small movie screen. "I got satellite hooked up," Junior says. "You wouldn't believe all the channels I can get."

"It's a nice set," Patterson says.

"It's a boring piece of shit," Junior says. "I been sitting here for three fucking hours trying to find something to watch that doesn't make me wanna take a pipe wrench to my own fingers. The only thing it doesn't have is *Wizard of Oz*, and that's the reason I fucking bought it."

Patterson takes a chair. "You get baseball games?"

"Yeah, I get baseball games. Everybody gets baseball games."

"Let's see a game."

Junior flips channels, stopping on a Reds game. "You want a drink?" he asks.

"I can't dance and it's raining too hard to haul stone."

"Is that a yes?"

"It means yes."

"Then say what you fucking mean." Junior fetches a couple of glasses and a bottle of bourbon out of the kitchen, hands one of the glasses to Patterson. "You don't happen to know any ladies with black hair, do you? About twenty years younger'n you? Better looking than you'd ever have any right to think about?"

"Not interested." Patterson takes the bottle and pours himself a drink. "And I hope that ain't what you brought me here for."

"Not hardly," Junior says.

"Then what?"

"You're going to want to finish your drink first," he says. "I can promise you that."

nagging

Chase is tied onto a ladder-backed kitchen chair in Junior's basement, clothesline triple-wrapped around each arm and leg, duct tape over his mouth. His tank top and jeans are stiff with dried blood and vomit, his face swollen and red. Patterson whistles softly, coming down the basement stairs, and Chase's eyes try to leap out of their sockets and strangle him.

"You got yourself into a hell of a mess," Patterson says to him.

"I wouldn't have duct taped his mouth except he kept screaming." Junior leans on the wall by the stairs. "Not that anybody could probably hear him on the street, but I could hear him over the television."

"One hell of a mess." Patterson kneels down in front of Chase. Chase's arms strain at the rope.

"I didn't know what you wanted me to do with him. He was nosing around Denver trying to figure out where you lived. Says you stole his drugs and ran off with his wife."

"He's full of shit," Patterson says. "He had his wife hogtied in the bathroom. When I let her loose she took all his crystal meth. I ain't seen her since." From the way the chair starts hopping up and down, Patterson can tell Chase doesn't believe him.

"He didn't come to do you any good. So you know. He had a little Kel-Tec .380 on him and there was a shotgun in his car."

"That right?" Patterson asks Chase. "You come to kill me?" Chase's head bobs up and down sharply. "Jesus," Patterson says.

"Shoot him," Junior says. "Nobody'll hear it. Hell, even if they do, nobody'll give a shit."

"I don't think he's going to give me much of a choice," Patterson says, impressed. Chase's head is still bobbing.

"I don't think he is," Junior says.

Patterson lifts his T-shirt and slides his .45 out of its holster, letting it sit on his leg loose in his hand. Chase starts grunting something in a furious chant, like pistons driving. Tears squirm out of his red eyes and stream down his cheeks, over the duct tape. "You want to say anything?" Patterson asks him. His chin jerks up and down. "Go ahead," Patterson says to Junior.

"If you yell out, you won't have to worry about him," Junior says to Chase. "I'll shoot you before you get the first syllable out." He rips the duct tape free of Chase's mouth, hard.

Chase's mouth works for a few seconds before he can speak. "I wasn't going to hurt that bitch," he croaks. "That's a game we play, you dumb cocksucker. She likes that shit."

"I oughtta shoot you for that lie alone," Patterson says.

"Fuck you," Chase says, his voice gaining strength. "You don't know how that bitch is. She nags and nags and fucking nags. Locking her in the bathroom is the only way you can get any peace at all."

Junior starts laughing.

"I don't see how that shit's funny. She could nag dogs off a meat truck." Chase's voice rises into a falsetto. "Chase, buy me a pack of cigarettes. Chase, let me hit that. Chase, fetch me one of them McMuffins. Chase, pick that shit up. Chase, get off my sister. Goddamn, could that bitch nag."

"You realize you told us two completely different stories right in a row," Patterson says. "Right like that, without even pausing."

"I ain't got time for this shit," Chase says.

"You came to Denver to kill me," Patterson says. "You ain't got any time at all."

"What the fuck ever," Chase says. "I didn't come to kill you. I come to get her back. I come to bring her home with me. I love the bitch."

"I don't have your wife," Patterson says. "I don't have your crystal meth either."

"I'm supposed to believe that?" Chase says. "I'm supposed to believe you found a naked woman in a tub that looked like that and you didn't run off with her? That you left a couple of thousand bucks' worth of crank there on the table?"

"Believe whatever you want," Patterson says. "I don't give a shit. I ain't got a reason in the world to lie to you."

Chase's chin starts trembling. Then his lower lip.

"Jesus fucking Christ," Junior says.

Chase tries to control himself, but it's like trying to hold down the cover on a pressure cooker. He blows in an eruption of tears and snot that lasts a good minute before he begins a stuttering series of gasps, each one lessening in intensity, until he's finally quiet.

"You need to convince me that you know I don't have your wife," Patterson says.

"I know you don't have my wife," he says, his voice melancholy, his eyes red and downcast.

"And that you won't be looking for her in Denver anymore," Patterson adds. "Hell, Colorado."

"I know it," Chase says. "I know she ain't here." His fists clench in their bonds. "Goddamn it."

"All right," Patterson says. He passes his .45 into his left hand, flips his clip knife out of his pocket, slices the ropes apart.

Chase rubs his wrists. "That shit hurts."

"C'mon." Patterson closes his knife on his leg, pockets it. "I'll stand you a tank of gas and some food."

"You're a soft touch," says Junior, starting up the stairs.

"I know it." Patterson turns to follow him.

That's when Chase hits Patterson over the head with the chair. The front and rear footrails splinter on Patterson's back and the leg stiles snap off, clattering on the floor. Patterson tries to spin, but Chase jumps on his back, clamping his teeth down on his shoulder. He claws for the gun, still in Patterson's left hand. Patterson shoots an elbow back, connects with something, pain ripping up his ulnar nerve. Chase chews shoulder muscle. Patterson lurches, rams his back into the cinder-block wall, and the man falls away. The basement wobbles around Patterson when he sees the blood drooling out of Chase's mouth.

"Shoot him," Junior says.

"You motherfucker," Chase spits at Patterson, blood flecking through the air. "I know you got her." He's crouched down on the balls of his feet.

"Will you shoot him?" Junior says.

Chase lunges at Patterson, making a screeching noise from the back of his throat. Patterson throws his left arm up, the one holding the .45, and Chase sinks his teeth into Patterson's forearm. He wraps his arms around Patterson and gnaws. Patterson slams his right fist into the side of Chase's head. Chase's legs slip out from under him, and they fall together to the floor. Patterson punches him again in the side of the head. Again. Chase's head bounces on the concrete floor. Patterson punches him again. Again. Again.

"Oh, for Christ's sake," Junior says, standing there watching. "Will you shoot him already?"

Patterson stands. Chase is crumpled up on the floor like something you'd leave discarded outside of a trailer-park dumpster.

"I'd have shot him," Junior says.

"He had his fucking teeth in the arm that was holding the gun," Patterson says.

"Switch hands."

"Switch hands. Fuck you."

"You broke his nose anyway."

Patterson sits down heavily on the floor. He hangs his head.

"Take a minute," Junior says. "I'll tie him back up. Unless you want to shoot him now?"

Patterson shakes his head. Then he isn't entirely there at all. He's in and out of a gray-black fog. He's looking for something, something he can't find. And it's terrifying him that he can't find it. And then he realizes it's his son, Justin. His full cheeks flushed, and one of his little fists balled up the way he did when he got scared. Patterson doesn't know how long it lasts, but when he comes awake he's still sitting on the floor and Junior is shaking his shoulder.

"You need something to eat," Junior says.

"Food," Patterson says thickly.

"Unless you want to go to the hospital," Junior says.

"Food."

edges

They walk to a corner bar by the stock-show complex where Junior says they'll still let you smoke cigarettes. It's original Denver, Italianate brick. A fat man sits at the bar next to a blond, cherub-faced lady with cheeks as pink as a drugstore rose, and off in one corner a tall cowboy sleeps at one of the low bar tables underneath a whorehouse nude. It's windowless, everywhere trimmed in red vinyl, the kind of place where old jackpot rodeo riders drink away the ones they couldn't ride and the ones that walked away.

The bartender is a fat woman, all of it rolling around in a dirty yellow sweat suit as she moves behind the bar. She microwaves frozen burritos for them, and while Junior shovels his into his mouth, Patterson stares at the bandagework on his arm, now and then trying to force down a bite. Then Junior finishes his food and flips open his cigarette pack. Empty. "You got any cigarettes?" he asks.

"I'm out," Patterson says.

Junior signals the bartender, points to their bottles of beer. "Two more, and a pack of cigarettes."

"We're out of cigarettes," she says, uncapping the beer. "There's a gas station down the street."

Junior tips his bottle at her and drinks, then looks over at Patterson. "How's the arm?"

"It hurts." Patterson's voice smears across the thick bar air. "Hurts like a son of a bitch."

"We got all kinds of antibiotics on it," Junior says. "And we wrapped the hell out of it. I don't think they could have done more at a hospital."

Patterson shrugs, his shoulders crumbling away like the foundation is sinking under them.

"You don't have to be embarrassed or nothing," Junior says.

"I'm not embarrassed."

"About almost fainting."

Patterson just manages not to pull his gun and shoot Junior in the teeth. "I didn't faint."

"I said almost."

"I didn't almost faint."

"You got a little light-headed there, partner," Junior says. "That's all I'm saying."

The bar door opens behind them and a hot streak of unwelcome sunlight cuts its way in on them. "Junior!" a woman squeals in an excited voice that rips a hole right through Patterson's head. "Junior Bascom!"

"Son of a bitch," Junior says under his breath. She's a big girl and there's a sort of burnt-crisp wrinkle to her face like there's a smoker working inside her, jerking her skin. The girl with her, though, she's different. Redheaded, high-titted, and good-looking in that malleable way strippers are, like the years of affecting desire have somehow plasticized their skin. Junior's wearing his eye patch and his good eye hops all over that one. "Hello, Darlene," he says to the big girl with a little more enthusiasm.

"Hello, Darlene," she mocks. "I ain't seen you in four years or more and that's all you got to say to me." She slaps his arm. "That's a sorry greeting, Junior."

"It's been a long day," Junior says.

"Well, you're looking good," she says. Her eyes flick over to Patterson. "Is this your dad?"

Junior barks out a laugh. Patterson reaches his hand out to her. The one without the bandages. If he were to move that one, he thinks he just might faint after all. "Patterson Wells."

She shakes his hand. "Good to meet you, Patterson Wells."

"What'll you have?" Junior asks, his eye straying. "For old times."

"Bud Light," Darlene answers. Behind her the redhead nods.

"Two Bud Lights," Junior says to the bartender, who is already picking them out of the cooler. "What are you doing in town?" he asks Darlene. "I thought you moved east after rehab. Syracuse or something."

Darlene takes a pack of Marlboro Menthol Lights out of her purse and eyeballs the empty pack in front of Junior. "You want one of mine?"

"Menthol?"

"Menthol."

Junior waves them off. "I don't smoke them niggerettes," he says.

Darlene slaps him on the arm. "My uncle died." She extracts a cigarette from the pack, nods at the redhead. "This is his daughter, Shawna."

"I'm sorry about your loss," Junior says to Shawna. Patterson manages to mumble something like that, too.

Shawna lights one of Darlene's cigarettes. She looks too young to smoke. She also looks like it probably ain't the first time. Watching Junior stare at her tits, Patterson wants to tell her to put a sweatshirt on. "Don't worry about it," she says.

"All right," Junior says. "I won't."

Darlene smacks him on the arm again. Something flashes across his face that she doesn't see. "Don't be mean to her," she says. "She's a good kid, and it ain't easy losing your father."

"I think it's real easy," Shawna says. "I ain't had any problem with it at all."

"Aw, honey." Darlene strokes her arm, her fingers trailing boozily. "You don't mean it."

Shawna lifts her eyebrows, drinking from the bottle of Bud Light. She seems like she means it to Patterson. Junior looks her over like she's a big piece of meat and he's deciding where to make the first cut.

"It ain't her fault," Darlene explains. "There's a lot of history between her and her old man."

"There's very little history," Shawna says. "There's almost no history at all."

"Well," says Darlene, "that's what I mean." She strokes the girl's hair. "Aw, honey," she says again. She turns to Junior, and the whole sorry mess, whatever it is, threatens to come spilling out of her mouth.

"Tell you what," Junior cuts her off. "Whyn't you pretend you already done told me all about it and I'll pretend I'm real sympathetic."

Darlene raises her hand to smack him in the arm again, but she doesn't miss his look this time. She giggles, deciding it's all in good fun. "You haven't changed a bit."

Shawna draws a pill bottle out of her purse. She unscrews the childproof cap, taps three of the pills into her palm, chases them down her throat with a swallow of her beer. Then she taps out three more and sets them on the bar in front of Darlene.

"I can't take those," says Darlene, watching the pills like they might start playing leapfrog across the bar. "I don't even know what they are."

"Percocet," Patterson says.

"You want a couple?" Shawna asks him.

Patterson smiles weakly, thinking he might just faint before her mercy. "Please."

She fishes out three more pills and hands them to him. Patterson chews them. "How about you?" she asks Junior.

"I got everything I need," says Junior.

Darlene's still holding the pills in her palm.

"They won't hurt you," Junior says. "Just take the edge off."

"I been drinking all day," says Darlene. "I ain't got any edges left."

"Then they'll help you sharpen them up a little," Junior says.

Darlene rolls the pills in her palm. "If I take them you ain't leaving, are you?"

"I ain't got nowhere to be," Junior says.

"All right." She places a lonely pill on her fat tongue, takes a hopeless drink of beer through her fat lips, washes it down her fat throat, swallows. She repeats the same for the following pill. By the third, none of them can look at her.

free

Darlene snores, her mouth slack, saliva pooling on the surface of the bar. Shawna empties her purse. Keys, a battered pen, a cell phone, a long-toted condom with a scuffed wrapper, a tube of lipstick. Then, finally, her pocketbook, which Shawna strips of six dollars and twenty or thirty coins. Pennies mostly, greenish and dull. "She doesn't have any credit cards," Shawna says with disgust. "Not a single fucking credit card."

"It ain't against the law," Junior says.

Shawna lets the coins fall out of the pocketbook, cascading in a clatter on the bar. "What kind of person doesn't have credit cards?"

"People who live off the grid," Patterson says. He's recovering a little with the help of the pain pills.

"What's that mean?" Shawna says. "Off the grid?"

"Weird motherfuckers," says Junior. "The kind who think aliens are out to get them. That 9/11 was an inside job. That the CIA invented crack-cocaine."

"That one's true," Patterson says. "Freeway Ricky Ross."

"I heard it the same place you did," Junior says.

"Living without leaving a paper trail," Patterson says. "No recorded address, no social security number, nothing the government can use to track you. Trying to be free."

Shawna sneers at her cousin. "Does that cow look like she cares about being free?"

Patterson looks at Darlene. Then he shakes his head.

Shawna sighs. "No credit card," she says. "Not fucking one. Not even a debit card." She picks up the scuffed condom, turns it over in her hand. She's biting her bottom lip, shaking her head to herself, like even she can't believe what it is she's about to do.

"You been looking at my tits," she says to Junior.

"All night." Junior nods agreeably. "They's hard to miss."

"You got money?"

"Yeah." He nods. "I got money."

"How much."

Junior removes his eye patch, and Patterson can tell he doesn't miss the way she winces, seeing his bad eye. "A couple of hundred bucks," he says.

"All right." She stands, holding the condom by the edge of the wrapper. "Women's bathroom. Let's go."

Junior tosses the eye patch on the bar and follows her.

Patterson sits alone at the bar trying not to think about the two of them. She can't be more than seventeen, and she'd buried her father that day. He knows that she said she didn't care, but nobody who says that means it. Not even Junior. Especially not Junior. It's like he considers something contemptible about a person who'd get abandoned by their own father. Like you've got to put people out of their misery when they have that kind of affliction. Patterson realizes he's clenching his fist, the one attached to his injured arm. And he realizes how hard it's throbbing, even through the Percocet. He relaxes it as slowly as he can.

Five minutes later, Junior's back, retaking his stool next to Darlene. She's still snoring, still drooling on the bar. Junior picks up his eye patch and strings it around his head. Patterson makes a pledge to himself to get back to Junior's house, untie Chase, and get the hell out of Denver.

Shawna pushes the door of the bathroom open with her toe. She walks over and stands next to Junior's stool, her face blanched but steady.

Junior finishes his beer. He doesn't look at her.

"All right," she says.

"All right," Junior says.

"All right. Let's have it."

Junior pulls out his wallet, flips through the few bills so that everyone can see. One twenty, two fives, three ones. He removes the twenty and places it on the bar next to his beer. "Keep the change," he says to the bartender. Then he tosses the rest of the bills on the bar for Shawna.

"Don't say it," she hisses, her free hand balled into a fist.

Junior turns back to his beer.

She walks around her cousin and sits down at the bar on the other side of her. "I knew it when I looked at you," she says. She covers her mouth with a handful of chipped pink nails.

"Pay attention to first impressions," Junior says, pulling one of Darlene's menthol cigarettes out of her pack. "That's my advice."

"Pick your hand up," the bartender says to Junior.

Junior lights his cigarette, the lighter flame haloing in the liquor fumes hanging in the air.

"Pick your hand up," the bartender says. "Off the bar. You've got shit on your hand."

Junior turns his arm and looks. Sure enough, a streak of shit down the flat of his hand. He stands, laughing, and heads back to the bathroom to wash it off.

Shawna waits until the bathroom door closes and then begins to cry.

Patterson opens his wallet and draws out two hundred dollars. "Here," he says, handing it to the girl.

home

When they leave the bar Patterson can't wait to be rid of Junior. To get back to the mesa, where he can open up his bandages and look at his wounds without Junior sitting over him. It's all he can think of as they walk back to Junior's, getting home. He figures to give Chase the best scare he can work up and cut him loose as quick as possible. That's what he's thinking.

But when they enter the basement Patterson stops thinking altogether.

Chase is slumped over in the chair, his head hung down on his chest and his body sagging against the ropes. Patterson stands and looks at him. If Junior wasn't there behind him he thinks he'd probably vomit. But Junior is, so Patterson takes Chase's chin in his hand and lifts his face. There's no doubt but that he's dead. His skin is yellowish, waxy, and the muscles droop lopsided so that his head slides a little, wobbling on top of his jaw.

"I'd say you hit him a little harder than maybe you meant to," says Junior.

Patterson wants to respond, but he can't. He thinks he makes some kind of grunt in the back of his throat, but he can't be sure.

"I'll get that bottle of bourbon," Junior says.

unraveling

Patterson's entire nervous system feels like it's unraveling right underneath his skin. It's the pain itself, and the Percocet for the pain, as Patterson lifts and tugs Chase's body onto the tarp, Junior helping. It's that Chase's body seems to keep rubbing the bandage on Patterson's arm, catching it and pulling it out of place. Patterson keeps trying to smooth it down, but that doesn't work. So he just tries to keep it away from Chase, which is next to impossible. And the little tweaker is covered in his own bodily fluids. It's like every orifice he has is trying to excrete all the crank at once. So it's that, too.

But mostly it's trying to locate what is now missing in Chase's face. What had been there but no longer is. Patterson has done this before, watched the face of a person for what is now missing. And when he's recovered bodies, which he has done often, that's what he always wonders. What had been there that he never did see? You can't know a person by what's left after they're dead.

He had done himself a disservice when Justin died. When he came back from the bathroom at the hospital and found him dead, he'd tried to commit the boy's face to memory. He'd stared at the strange wax-colored ruin of his son, and he was so scared that he might forget something about him that he wouldn't let himself blink. He stared at Justin's face until he knew he wouldn't forget him no matter what he did.

And he couldn't. That was the problem. It took years before he could remember the boy's face without it being in that hospital bed, wax-colored and strange. Photographs didn't help. They never do. The only thing that brought his son back to him was time. Time and writing in the notebooks.

Then they have Chase wrapped up in the tarp. And Junior is sitting on the stairs, lighting a cigarette. "Don't tell me you're gonna start crying about the little fucker."

Patterson's heart swells. Swells with hatred. And then he realizes that Junior's not talking about Justin, but about Chase. Which is, of course, the only thing he could be talking about. He thinks of Chase on the job, then. Working the chipper, singing along to the radio, but fucking up the lyrics. The first one to buy a beer, the first one to tell a joke on himself. He had the kind of loose way with his own self that Patterson never did.

"He probably deserves better than he got," Patterson says.

"Nobody deserves better than they got," Junior returns.

Patterson runs his hand over his bandage, carefully around the bite, thinking that he should get rid of it. That no good can come from wearing it after wrapping up the body. It's brown and yellow and crusted all over with Chase. Patterson can only guess at the amount of forensic evidence on that bandage. And he tugs at a loose end of it, which pinches his wound. He grunts in pain. Then he remembers that the bandage is there because Chase has bitten him. And there's nothing in that bandage that isn't already in his wound.

This time he has to hold himself up against one of the walls of the basement. And he has to do that for a long time.

Right up until Junior says, "You want a quick bump?"

coyotes

The one thing unincorporated Adams County is not short of is places to bury a body. They find one of the many large and vacant lots in between the refinery and the rendering plant, and dig a hole in a grove of cottonwoods. They've been keeping their courage up with thick lines of cocaine, and are both a little twitchy and flushed. "Think that's deep enough?" Junior asks finally, leaning on his shovel and spitting down into the hole.

"Hell if I know," Patterson says. Between the cocaine and the Percocet, he's feeling no pain now.

"Looks to me like we're a good three to four feet down. That's got to be deep enough."

"There's body-sniffing dogs," Patterson says.

"Somebody has to think there's a body out here to bring body-sniffing dogs."

"There's coyotes, too. Plenty of coyotes."

"You ever known a coyote to dig down into four feet of dirt?"

"Still. I wish we'd thought to bring some quicklime."

"It'll be all over in a minute," Junior says. "He'll be in the ground and won't nothing dig him up."

Patterson looks at him.

"How's about we toss the body in the hole?" Junior says. "How's about we just bury the motherfucker?"

Patterson nods. He pulls the tarp-wrapped carcass out of the bed of the truck by the head, Junior takes it by the feet, and together they heave it at the hole. It lands tipping half in and half out and they kick it the rest of the way in. Then they fill the hole and cover it with enough grass, dirt, and cottonwood branches to disguise it, at least by their midnight account. "We should have brought clothes," Patterson says, throwing his shovel in the back of the truck.

"Should have, would have, could have."

"Clothes and some water to wash up with. We got mud all over us. My truck's going to have evidence everywhere."

"I can loan you some jeans and a T-shirt when we get back to my place. And bleach for the truck bed." Junior lights a Marlboro, the flame illuminating his face in a sudden yellow and orange burn that collapses on itself as quick as it came, leaving nothing but a red imprint burned into Patterson's retina. He passes him a cigarette and his lighter. "That the first grave you've ever dug?"

"I've dug bodies out before," Patterson says. "Out of rubble." He lights his cigarette. "How about you?"

Junior shakes his head.

Patterson sags against the truck. "Probably do it all the time. Meth dealer and all."

"Just the once," Junior says.

"Which once?"

"When I was a kid."

The whole scene shifts sideways in front of Patterson's eyes like a television flickering. He has to force himself to focus on Junior's face. On his bad eye. He's taken off the eye patch and liquid's running out of it and through the caked dirt on his face. "All right," Patterson says, against his own will. "Who?"

"It was an aneurysm that killed her, in her sleep," he says, and Patterson lets his eyes drop off Junior, trying not to show the relief on his face. He doesn't know what Junior was about to tell him, but he's more than happy to take an aneurysm. "She woke up dead," Junior continues. He looks around. "Where'd that bourbon go?"

"We drank it."

"We drank it," he repeats. "Henry lost his shit. He was coming off a weeklong whites and booze binge. He curled up in the corner, crying that he was the one who'd done it, cutting his arms all over with his Buck knife. Tells me I was an accomplice because I hadn't called the police. So we drove the body out to a field and I dug a grave and rolled her in it while he lay passed out in the backseat of the car."

Patterson doesn't bother trying to think of anything to say to that. He just closes his eyes and pretends he's somewhere else.

"The worst part was the next day when he'd figured out how fucking stupid he was. He made me dig her up again and clean her off, naked and everything. Then we took her back to the house and put her in bed." Junior spits on the ground. "Of course the cops knew exactly what we'd done the minute they saw her. You don't want to know the kind of mess that dumb fucker was after that, partner."

"No," Patterson says. "I don't."

"Let's head back to my house and get cleaned up," Junior says.

Justin

I drove through Denver yesterday, right through downtown. The last time I was up that way, I had you with me. I was taking you to a Rockie's game at Coors Field. If I know myself, I told you about my teenage dreams of making the major leagues myself. Which for a little while looked almost possible. At least until I made varsity and saw what mediocre-to-good players actually looked like. It was about then that I gave up on baseball fantasies and started running with an entirely different crowd. As I recall, though, you weren't exactly taken with the game, but you enjoyed the hell out of the play area and Dinger.

It's been a long time since I saw downtown Denver. When I was a kid, people didn't go downtown. It was flophouses and pool halls, half-destroyed brick industrial buildings taken over by addicts and bums. Now it's boutique shops and high-end restaurants, all the winos and junkies having been truncheoned out of the shopping district and spread up and down Colfax Avenue, where there's always room for more.

I spent a weekend in Las Vegas with a waitress once. She was one of maybe three women on Earth who could've talked me into spending a weekend in Vegas, and even so, we didn't survive it. From the minute I stepped off the plane I felt like I was getting smothered with a pillowcase, one with a thousand thread count that had been soaked in hairspray. It could never exist naturally, that city. It's like some kind of colony on the moon, only kept afloat by life support. If the food transport, climate control, or water pipelines were to fail, people would be dying in the streets in a matter of hours. It's a disaster waiting to happen. And one you couldn't pay me enough to work.

The thing is, Denver's not really any different. It looks like it is because there's grass on the plains, a couple of creeks running through town puffed up as rivers, and the occasional cottonwood or creek willow. But it's still the high desert. The population's exploding, the shopping districts are packed, every lawn has Kentucky bluegrass, and it's only a matter of time before the water runs out. When the crash happens I just hope I'm back on the mesa.

I was passing through LoDo just as the bars were getting out on the way home, and it was even worse than I'd imagined. Women in short skirts, walking with their shoes in their hands, their eyes and noses swollen with booze and bar hysteria. Men sidling sideways next to them, falling over each other. The smell of unisex body wash and fruit-flavored martinis blowing out from the clubs. It was like they were somehow living about four inches off the ground.

I've made some very poor choices lately, but I made it a point not to think about those as I drove. I knew I had to hold off on those until I got home.

ghosts

The next day, after cleaning out the bites on his arm and shoulder, neither of which look infected, and burning the bandages, Patterson sets his galvanized tub up in the living room and takes a bath. A long one, letting the water soak the pain out of the bites, watching the rumpled edges left by Chase's teeth pucker and whiten. He leaves the windows open so he can hear the birds, and, still in the bathtub, he eats a three-pound bloody steak with his hands. Then he dresses the wounds and drinks a bottle of George Dickel whiskey, reading on the porch. Every time he thinks of Chase he reads another poem and takes another drink. He retreats into the dark woods and ghosts of Robert Frost. Sancho, he sits by Patterson's side the whole time, like he's protecting him.

Chase and Patterson hadn't been great friends. Patterson knows he can't really claim that. Chase was weird even before the meth. He'd long gone a little crazy from being too broke, from hustling too hard for what little he had, from the vague sense that there was an entire world out there, conspiring against him. The type's easy to spot. The swagger, the chip on the shoulder, the rants about rich motherfuckers over here and stuck-up bitches over there.

But he had been some kind of friend, at least for the last season. He had the capability of being quiet. He wasn't great at it, but he could do it. And if Patterson needed to talk about something he read in a book, Chase would listen. He was always a little awed by the fact that Patterson read books, and Patterson can't say that he ever got the feeling Chase understood anything he was talking about, but he would listen. He sure as hell didn't deserve to be buried in a dirt patch in unincorporated Adams County. That's one thing Patterson knows.

Still, Patterson can't say he feels bad exactly about what happened to Chase. He hadn't gone looking for trouble, and Chase had been gnawing a chunk out of Patterson's arm when Patterson hit him, so it's hard to feel too guilty. But Patterson feels bad that they'd had to do that to him, just bury him out there.

Sitting there reading Robert Frost, Patterson makes himself some promises. Like to not get pulled into Junior's bullshit anymore. Patterson still doesn't know how in the hell he ended up as far in as he did. The first trip made sense, telling him to back off Henry. But then to get called back to scare Chase off, and then to have Chase end up dead, Patterson could have done without that. Junior could have left that one alone, could have let the little asshole go bowlegged and blind trying to hunt Patterson in Denver.

And, of course, Patterson could have left it alone himself. He could have left it alone all the way back to Chase's house in St. Louis. All the way back to Chase's wife. How the fuck do you chart choices that end up that bad?

. . .

A few hours after he's finished the bottle of bourbon, Patterson comes awake to the sound of a car pulling down the driveway. And when he lifts his Avrilla cap off his eyes, Laney is standing on the stairs of the porch, holding Gabe's hand. Patterson starts coughing, coughing hard, hacking phlegm into his fist. When he's done, he wipes his hand on the leg of his jeans and lights a cigarette. Then he holds the cigarette off to the side of his mouth to protect it while he coughs some more.

"Long night?" Laney asks, looking at the bandage on his arm.

"They're all long." Patterson grins a grin that he means to be rakish, but he's pretty sure it just comes off as gutshot.

"Looks like it," she says, looking pointedly at the bandage on his arm. Looking pointedly at things is something she does very well.

"It was a jackrabbit. Son of a bitch attacked me."

"Were you able to take care of it?"

"I took care of it, all right. Don't you worry about it."

She shakes her head. "We're having a picnic dinner," she says. "We've got fried chicken. I made it myself."

"Yeah?" Patterson has the feeling he's supposed to remember something about her fried chicken, but he doesn't. "How'd you know I was here?"

"I didn't," she says. "We were on our way up to the Sand Dunes. Gabe wants to play in Medano Creek."

"Is there still water? I thought it was dried up by now."

"It's still flowing. We checked on the internet."

"You checked on the internet?"

"Poor Patterson," she says. "Everything's on the internet. I could probably see if you're home on the internet. I could probably find a satellite image of your house and check if the truck's in the driveway."

The idea doesn't appeal to him. He looks up at the sky and winces as he catches sun in all that blue. "I could go with you," he says.

"Just a picnic," she says.

"Just a picnic." Patterson looks at the boy. He's small for his age, with black hair and a sharp face. A kind of strange and wary intelligence sunk deep down in his eyes. "You seen the horses?" Patterson asks him.

The boy shakes his head.

"There's a herd of web-footed horses that hide in the dunes."

"Stop it," Laney says.

"It's true," Patterson says. "I heard it on the radio. Brother Joe."

"I said stop it."

"How's about the gator farm?" Patterson says. "That's my favorite. It started as a tilapia farm, but the owners decided they'd buy a gator to eat the tilapia remains. Then they thought that gator might be lonely, so they bought another to keep him company. And now they have a gator farm and no tilapia at all. They wrestle them."

"I mean it," Laney says.

"That one's true," Patterson says, chuckling. "All right, then. There's another one. You can sled on the dunes. We'll stop in Alamosa and pick one up at the Walmart." He tries to stand, but his legs fail him on the first attempt. "And I'm going to need some beer."

Laney opens her mouth as if to say something to that. But she doesn't.

water

Patterson watches her ass as she walks from her bed to the bathroom. He can remember when he liked to watch her ass in the early days of their marriage. Turns out that given enough time even the most unlikely things'll come back to you. She closes the bathroom door quietly, a strip of yellow light streaking across the bottom. Patterson stays in bed and smokes, ashing into a beer bottle on the nightstand. Then the door opens and she returns to bed, sliding under the blanket and skinnying backward against him, fish-cold against his bare legs. "It was nice watching you two sled this afternoon," she says. "I didn't even know you could do that on the dunes."

Patterson grunts noncommittally. Gabe is a strange boy. A daydreamer who doesn't speak unless spoken to, and sometimes not even then. He isn't anything like Justin at all. They'd only made it up the dunes twice with the sled before he wanted to go back to the creek and his mother.

"All right," she says. She leans across Patterson to the end table, takes one of his cigarettes, and lights it. Then she sinks back down on her pillow, exhaling smoke. "Did you hear about Antonio?"

"Antonio who?"

"Antonio, our neighbor. My neighbor. Who you got drunk with on his porch whenever you got mad at me." She's lisping a little. She has a slight lisp that only shows up after her fourth drink. It's the sort of thing that was endearing in her twenties, less so now.

"I've been gone awhile," Patterson reminds her.

"His wife had to have her kidney removed," she says.

"Hadn't heard it."

She turns on her elbow, facing him. "You should stop by and say something to him."

"Like what?"

"Like offer to help out if he needs it. Like be a friend. His kids aren't well either. The little one, his bones are, what do you call it, dissolving."

"Deteriorating."

"That's it. Deteriorating."

"They shouldn't be drinking the tap water." Patterson drops the butt of his cigarette in the beer bottle he'd been ashing in.

She stays on her elbow, watching him. Her eyes liquid red in the light of her cigarette coal. "They say you should drink eight glasses of water a day," she says.

"As close as you are to the molybdenum mine, you'd be dead in a year," Patterson says. "I haven't had a glass of water since we got divorced."

"I don't doubt it." She reaches out with her cigarette hand, strokes his arm for a minute. "It was nice, I mean really nice, to see you and him on the dunes."

Patterson grunts.

"All right," she says. She's silent for a moment. "I've been thinking," she says.

Patterson has an urge to get up and leave right there. "About what?"

"About leaving Questa. About moving someplace where you can drink the tap water."

"Well. Where would you go?"

"Denver, maybe. It doesn't have to be far. You can drink the tap water most places."

"You can't drink the tap water anywhere," Patterson says. "I was just in Denver and you can't even breathe the air."

She finishes her cigarette and passes him the butt. He drops it in the empty beer bottle on his side of the bed. "Did you see Gabe's hands?" she asks. "While you were sledding?"

He grunts.

"I mean it," she says. "His hands shake. And he gets headaches."

"Don't let him drink the tap water," Patterson says.

"That's all you have to say?" she says. "Don't let him drink the tap water?"

Patterson folds the sheet off and swings out of the bed.

"Oh, fuck you," she says. "Get back in bed."

"I have to get up early."

"That's bullshit," she says. "Get back in bed. I'll quit talking."

Patterson pulls his jeans on in the dark. "No you won't." He kisses her on the forehead. "I really do have to get up early."

It isn't exactly true, but he does have to get out of that bedroom.

tattoos

Patterson starts work for Paulson, clearing brush for home pads. He has no intention of following Henry's plans for him, but he knows he could always use a little more money. Besides which, clearing brush is hard work, but it's not dangerous in the way climbing trees is. And Patterson gets the feeling Paulson wouldn't mind having someone to manage his Mexicans. It's something about the way he turns his head away from them to spit in the dirt after he gives an order. That could mean spending the summer sitting in the cab of his truck, getting paid to watch other people work.

They can work, though. Patterson does everything he can to keep up with them and puts in a solid fourteen hours doing it. The wounds left him by Chase don't bother him much anymore, but by the end of the day, all his old tree-trimming aches have returned. He can barely walk without clutching his lower back, his left hand is swollen to the size of a baseball glove, and there's black patches smearing across his vision from the pain in his shoulder. He's still paying for the things he did to his body ten years ago, and there's times it threatens to all gang up together and cripple him completely.

For his part, Sancho spends the entire day lying in the dirt and watching him work. Patterson gets the feeling Sancho would like nothing better than to move to the mesa full-time.

Then, when he pulls up to the cabin, there she is again. Laney, sitting on the front porch reading. "I got a babysitter," she says, shutting her book. "Where have you been? You're supposed to take me out."

Patterson kicks the furniture around in his memory, but he can't find any conversation that would indicate that.

"Relax," she says. "What I mean is that I drove up here hoping you would take me out."

"Got it."

Her eyes narrow. "So where have you been?"

There doesn't seem any point in trying to hide it now, so Patterson answers. "Working."

"Working?"

"Henry got me a job," Patterson says. "He's trying to convince me to move onto the mesa full-time."

Her eyes widen. "Oh, Jesus," she says. "Look at you."

"I'm fine," Patterson says. And he doesn't vomit blood when he says it, which is a kind of achievement in itself.

She sets her book on the floor and comes down off the porch. "I'm sorry," she says. "I'll help."

"It'll be easier tomorrow," Patterson says. "That's the thing about getting old. It's always easier tomorrow."

She takes him by the arm. "Here," she says, leading him inside and to the couch. "Here. What do you usually do?"

"Get drunk," Patterson says.

She looks at him.

"There's some Bengay under the sink," Patterson says. "I ain't asking, though."

Come dark, he's laid out on the tattered blanket on the floor of the cabin and she's giving him a Bengay rubdown by lamplight. "Did you know Henry talks to his wife?" she asks, prodding at his sunburnt flesh like she's performing some kind of surgery with her fingers.

"When did you and Henry get to be such good friends?"

"We talk on the phone," she says, simply.

"About what?"

"This and that. He's interesting."

"Sure," Patterson wheezes, all the strength in his lungs being drawn out by her hands. "And, no, he's never told me he talks to his wife."

"He does, all the time. He's got her ashes in his trailer. He says she answers him, too."

"Bet her voice sounds just like his," Patterson says.

She digs so hard into his shoulders that he almost whimpers. "Don't make fun of him," she says, and her voice isn't entirely friendly.

"I'm not," Patterson says. Then he has a thought. "Did he tell you how she died? His wife?"

"Some kind of cancer," she says. "It took a long time, half a year. He sat with her in the hospital."

"That's what he told me, too. I always thought it was from drinking the water."

This time she smacks the back of his head. "Why'd you ask?" she says.

"I heard another story about it, too," Patterson says.

"You heard it from the asshole, his son," she says. "Henry's told me about him. Says that you and he have struck up quite a friendship."

"I wouldn't call it that," Patterson says.

"Henry's changed," she says. "People change."

"Junior remains unconvinced."

She digs again. This time he does whimper. "Junior's wrong," she says.

"I ain't arguing with you," Patterson says.

"Did you thank Henry for getting you this job?" she asks.

"I need to load my gun first."

"I'm done," she says. But she doesn't move. Her fingers skimming lightly over his back, then down his arms. "I can see them now," she said. "The tattoos. The ones you tried to cover up. It's funny that I couldn't see them when we were married."

"Some people see them right away," Patterson says. "It takes others longer."

"Why did you get them?"

"They were free. And they scared people."

"Did you really beat up people? Just because of who they were?"

"Sometimes. Less than we beat up each other."

She shudders. "What about this?" she asks, feeling a lump under his right shoulder blade.

"Don't know," Patterson says. "I was pulling a hanger a couple of years ago and a branch speared me. Knocked me twenty feet down to the ground. That rose up about six months later."

"How don't you know? Didn't you go to the doctor?"

"Yeah, I went. Broke three ribs. But my mind was on other things."

"You broke three ribs and your mind was on other things? What was your mind on?"

"Every time you get injured on the job working for Avrilla you gotta get a drug test. I was pretty sure I wouldn't pass, so I got a buddy on the crew to piss for me in an Elmer's Glue bottle, and I taped it to my leg. The bottle leaked, and that's all I could think about while the doctor was talking. This other dude's piss dribbling down my leg."

She tries to say something, but she's laughing too hard.

"Get up," Patterson says. "I need a drink."

She rolls off him and waves helplessly for him to get her one, too.

As he lifts the whiskey bottle out from underneath the cabinet, there's a knock on the door. Patterson sighs, sits the bottle down, and opens it.

It's Emma. Standing in the doorway with her hands in the pockets of her Carhartt jacket. Looking as miserable as only a girl of her age can look. It's beginning to rain, droplets of water running down her hair and over her lightly freckled face, which is as washed-out as a farmhouse dishrag. Patterson takes her by the shoulder and guides her inside. "Come inside," he says. "Come on in."

Laney's already moving to them. She ushers Emma inside, removing her wet coat.

Patterson begins to pull his boots on. "There's some tea in the cupboard," he says. "She might like some."

"Where are you going?" Laney asks.

"I'll be back shortly," he says, belting on his holster.

cure

The door to Henry's cabin is unlocked. He's at the tack trunk in the living room, a single-action .44 magnum revolver next to a bottle of Old Crow that's three-quarters of the way empty, a glass in his left hand.

"The Jim Harrison heartbreak cure," Patterson says. "I had one of those earlier this week. The tub and the bloody steak, the whole bit."

"I'm the one who told you about it," Henry says.

"True enough. It's been a hell of a summer for your drinking."

"It's been a hell of a summer," he says, without looking at Patterson.

Patterson nods. "Why don't you let me have the gun?"

"Not yet." His right hand moves over to the .44. "I haven't made up my mind yet."

"You called Emma to get me," Patterson says. "That means you've made up your mind."

His eyes are bloodshot, a film of sweat over his face. "I called her to tell her I wasn't gonna be worth a shit tomorrow. I didn't call her to get me a babysitter."

"Well. She's with Laney."

"Good."

Patterson pulls out his cigarettes. "You mind if I smoke?"

"Go ahead," he says.

Patterson takes a saucer for an ashtray from one of his cabinets and sits down at the tack trunk. "You did everything you could," he says. "Laney and I were just talking about it."

Henry clears his throat. He drinks.

"She was sick." Patterson lights his cigarette. He watches Henry over the smoke.

"There was nothing I could do," Henry says.

"You can't fight cancer."

Henry clears his throat again. "She tried. She put everything she had into it. And I sat with her right up until the end."

"I know."

"What do you do, Patterson?" Even as drunk as he is, his voice is deep and clear, seeming to emanate out of the cedar paneling on the walls. "What do you do when you miss your son?"

"I write to him," Patterson says. "I try to feel him around me. Sometimes I get drunk with a loaded gun nearby."

"I don't want to talk anymore. And I don't want to give you my gun."

"You don't have to do either."

"I want to finish this bottle and then go to bed."

"You mind if I sit here with you?"

Henry shakes his head.

Patterson thinks of what Laney had said, about Henry talking to his wife. And Patterson can't help but wonder why Henry never told him about it. But it doesn't really matter. Patterson doesn't know what Henry says when he talks to her, but he knows what happens when she stops talking back.

Most of Henry's bad nights are like that. Patterson's not even sure anybody but Henry could call them bad. Come to think, Patterson's not sure most people would call most of his own bad nights bad. At least up until when he met Junior. He's broadened Patterson's horizons some. And sitting there by Henry, Patterson realizes how ridiculous Junior's story of his mother's death sounds. His burying her and then digging her back up. Which leads Patterson to thinking how ridiculous Junior seems in his entirety.

He sits with Henry until he finishes the bottle, and then he helps him get into bed. Henry's long past drunk, and he mumbles something when Patterson closes the door to his bedroom. Patterson's been his friend long enough that he doesn't ask him to repeat himself when drunk, so he unloads the .44 and sets the rounds next to the gun on the top shelf of his writing desk where Henry keeps his cleaning rods and oil. And then he slips the whiskey bottle into the trash and washes out his glass.

late

There's times when Junior needs to be alone. It's one of the reasons he doesn't live with Jenny, that he pays rent on two houses on the same block instead. Most days he gets along with people as well as anybody, but there are some when his skin seems to crawl off his body altogether, exposing his nervous system to the outside world. On those days, he stays gone. He doesn't do other people's company. Or, at least, the company of people he knows.

It's been like that a lot lately.

This morning he wakes up in the front seat of his car, his mouth hanging open, tasting something between a gravel quarry and a cotton gin. The last thing he remembers is I-25, coming back from his second run in a row down to the border. He knows he should remember more, but that's it. Thoughts, they're beginning to slip.

It takes a few minutes for him to peel his eyelids open. And a few more for the morning sun to back off him enough that he can make anything out. Parking lot, back of a biker blues bar on Thirty-Eighth, near Federal. Must have been a hell of a night. Junior gets his hand into the breast pocket of his shirt, finds his cigarettes and lighter.

He lights one, exhaling the smoke in a ragged stream. And he feels his stomach swell and tighten with guilt. Knowing that every run to the border he makes, every morning he wakes up unfit to see Casey, is one more thing he won't be able to make up to her. And that makes him want to find Henry and stomp his head into the ground.

Then he notices the girl beside him in the passenger's seat. A denim skirt too short and a white T-shirt too thin, her pale face dented and stained like an old piece of drywall. She's wearing Junior's eye patch, but it's been shoved over onto her nose in her sleep. Junior tugs it off her head, not entirely gently, but she doesn't even stir. He puts it on and, thinking of Casey again, gives the girl's shoulder a shove with his elbow. Her eyes flutter and consciousness comes to her body in jerks, like power returned to some ancient robotic toy. "Glad you're alive," Junior says.

"Oh, fuck," she says. And she sounds like she means it. Then her arms spasm, and her eyes go wide. "What time is it?"

"Hell if I know."

Her hands flap around behind her, beside her. "Where's my purse?" She finds it on the floorboard, flips it open. "Oh, fuck. He's called seventeen times."

"Who?"

"Lem."

"Your pimp?"

"Fuck you." She closes the cell phone. "Yes."

"Where'd I pick you up?"

"Colfax. East Colfax."

"Do I owe you any money?"

"Yes. No. I don't think so."

"Good," Junior says. "Let me finish this cigarette and I'll drive you back. He'll get over it."

She shakes her head, her bottom lip trembling. She looks for all the world like a little girl. Which she is. "He knows where I am," she says miserably. "There's a GPS transmitter in my phone. He tracks me on his laptop."

"I'll be a son of a bitch," Junior says admiringly. "The things they can do with computers these days."

"Drive," she says. "You've gotta drive. We've gotta get back. You don't know what he'll do if he has to come after me."

"Jesus Christ," Junior says. "Hold on." He pats at his pockets for his keys. Nothing. On the floorboards. He reaches down to fetch them.

"Too late," she says in a quavering voice, and Junior hears a car door slam.

Lem's at the window when Junior raises his head up. His chest is sunken and knotted with bone, his hooded sweatshirt hanging open, a red beard that looks more like shaggy dream than reality. Junior opens the door hard and Lem has to jump backward to avoid getting hit.

"Sorry, partner," Junior says, standing out of the car. "Didn't see you there."

"Bitch," Lem spits at the girl. His hand sweeps around to his back. Junior doesn't wait to see what he has. He hurtles himself into Lem, and they fall back together into the blacktop, the back of Lem's head thudding on the asphalt, teeth clattering. It's a knife he's trying to pull, a Buck with a six-inch blade. Junior clamps down on his wrist and punches him in the face. "Fuck you." Lem spits blood and a piece of his tongue, bouncing off Junior's cheek. Junior pounds him in the face. Things slip out of place under his fist. Lem grabs Junior by the back of the neck, yanks him down for a head butt. Junior obliges, driving his forehead into Lem's nose, Lem's head into the asphalt. Then he grabs Lem's right ear and rips down and off.

"Goddamn," Junior says, holding the ear, skin hanging in tatters, blood draining from the fruitlike thing in his fist onto Lem's face. Blood roars in Junior's ears, the ground tilts.

"Goddamn," Junior says again, letting go of Lem's knife hand, waffling to his feet. Lem stays where he is. Curled into himself, blood running out of the hole in his head.

"Did you see that?" Junior says to the girl, who is out of the car, standing by the door, covering her mouth. She moves the hand covering her face away from her mouth, and, almost delicately, vomits down the front of her shirt.

Which clues Junior that it might be time to leave.

highlands ranch

Back home, it takes Junior a little time to get steady. But when he can, he takes a shower, changes into fresh clothes, and drags a kitchen chair out on his deck. He watches the thin clouds drift like gauze across the sun, doing nothing but not thinking about his life. There's a bleak and blackeyed current washing under the exhaustion that he knows better than to think he can sleep off.

Then Junior does something he does sometimes when he feels like this. He lifts the eye patch off his bad eye and moves it over so that it covers the good one. The bad eye fills with wincing pain at the light. But then that pain fades away, and there's just those high, thin clouds and his patchy backyard.

And, as always, Junior's not sure there's even a difference in the way he sees through the two. Except maybe things are a little softer through the bad eye. Like maybe the edges on things aren't quite so sharp. But he can never tell for sure. Even moving the patch back and forth, or covering one eye with one hand and then the other.

So he leaves the eye patch over his good eye and lets the day drift. Finally night falls, snuffing the hot sun. A few muggy stars swim around him in the smog. He doesn't know what the hell it is, but there's a knot in his chest like somebody's driven a baseball bat down his throat, barrel first.

Then Jenny opens the gate and comes into the backyard. "Hi," she says. She's carrying a six-pack of Budweiser longnecks. She hands him one.

"Where's Casey?" he asks.

"Mom's sitting with her. They're watching a movie." She sits down cross-legged on the deck floor and looks up at him. She tries not to look at his bad eye, but her lips tighten. "It looks good," she says, looking away from him. "The deck."

"Nothing's level," he says. "Nor even."

"It looks good," she says again. Her eyes are hooded in the semi-light, she seems to be peering out at him through the mask of her own face. Then she says, "We need to talk."

"About what?"

She pulls in a breath. Then lets it out slowly. "We're moving."

Junior can't talk for a minute. Something rises up in his diaphragm that closes off his ability to say anything. "Where?"

"Highlands Ranch."

He removes the eye patch and restrings it over his bad eye. "What the hell are you going to do in Highlands Ranch? The last time I drove through, I got pulled over three times for looking suspicious. Damn near came back the next day and set somebody's gate on fire."

"You do look suspicious," she says.

"Well."

"I have a job," she says. "A job and an apartment."

It occurs to him that Highlands Ranch is as far away from him as you could get and still be in Denver, and he feels a little like the earth's moving out from under him.

"Hey," she says. She puts her hand on his arm. "Hey."

"All right." He shakes her hand off his arm. "I'll still give you money. The same money I give you now."

"You don't have to do that," she says. "And you can come by as much as you want. You can see her whenever you have time."

He can't talk for a little bit. The beer's rising in his throat now, smothering his voice. Then, "What are they watching?" he asks. "Her and your mom?"

"*Wizard of Oz*," she answers. "Do you want to go sit with them?"

"Yeah," he says. "I do." He rises, a little too quickly. He has to step forward to keep from falling, the sole of his cowboy boot slapping on the deck. He rights himself.

"Easy," she says. She takes him by the arm, supports him. "Steady."

Justin

I know I've never told you much about your grandparents. That's mainly because there ain't much to tell. They were pretty well crushed under their lives by the time I was born. Your grandmother, she had some idea of being a singer when she was younger. A folksinger, I think. She still had a guitar when I was a kid, and she'd play me songs. Probably the same songs I sang to you, old cowboy songs she learned from Ramblin' Jack Elliott records.

That's how she met your grandfather, singing in a bar where she was pushing beer in between sets. He was straight off the plane from Vietnam, splintered all over with finally being free of it. I've always thought that's what drew her to him. Disillusioned Vietnam veterans, they were in high demand toward the end of the war.

It didn't work out for either of them, of course. He found he wasn't free of anything, and having your own Vietnam vet turned out to be inadequate for starting a career on the folksinger circuit. Especially when it wasn't much of a circuit anymore. She was still trying to sing acoustic Dylan a decade after he'd gone electric.

By the time I came along they were a couple of drunks. Not drinkers, drunks. Your grandmother was working as a nurse in a rest home and your grandfather a security guard. When they got home from work, they tried to do normal shit. Make dinner, help me with homework, straighten up the house. But the minute they felt they were done with it, they turned on the television and got drunk.

They must've loved each other, though. They didn't seem to need anybody else, at least. They didn't have any friends at all that I recall. Of course, they fought all the time, and for no reason at all. I remember them nearly getting into a fistfight over a moon landing documentary on PBS one night. Your grandfather swearing up and down that the whole thing was faked, your grandmother yelling at him that she didn't want him filling my head with that kind of bullshit.

I didn't understand them at all. I still don't. They gave me a lot of room to move as a kid, and I took advantage of it. I made friends easy, and there always seemed to be something to do outside of the house. There was a gang of kids with similarly useless parents, and we'd spend all day smoking cigarettes, hustling around the alleyways of East Denver, raiding our neighbors' garages for their beer. Then I started playing baseball and there was no reason to ever show up at home again. And I sure as hell wasn't welcome after they saw what I'd turned into once I gave up on that.

I don't think I ever really thought about them as people until Dad shot himself. It was a little before you were born that he drove down by the river, trying to keep Mom from finding him, and put a bullet from his 1911 into his temple. I was in North Carolina and drove straight back for the funeral.

Sitting out on the porch of their house with my mom, I tried to ask her about it. What there was that I didn't know that would make him unhappy enough to do that. I was trying to be delicate, because I didn't know if the answer was her, so I don't think I asked the question very well. At least that's what I got from her answer. You don't have to be particularly unhappy to shoot yourself, was what she said. Your average life will do it. Which she followed by finishing her glass of wine and pouring herself another. And it was only a couple of years later that her memory started to go.

Anyway, I finally visited her today. That had to be done. I was actually pretty proud of myself, in that it's usually well into July before I make it over there. Of course, she didn't know me from the janitor. She never does, anymore. Used to be she'd think I was your grandfather, but there's not even that left in her. She just lays there in her bed, her mouth open like a fish, while I hold her hand and watch television.

It was your mother, Laney, who insisted we put her in the home in Taos. I was for letting her stay in Denver, figuring there was a kind of justice in her spending her golden years in the same shit-hole where she'd worked. But your mother and I never have shared a sense of humor. She told me not to be an asshole, and I guess she was right. At least now I don't have to drive all the way to Denver to visit her.

It was your mother who reminded me to go see her today, if you want the truth. She called me this morning, right after sunrise. And she asked me to stop by her house afterward. That I owed her that, to see the paperwork, at least. That I wasn't the only one working through this. That she couldn't sleep nights for knowing what Dr. Court could do to somebody else's child. That I could donate the money or do whatever I wanted with it. That I owed it to her, to sit down in her kitchen with the papers in front of me and make a decision.

Of course, I promised to be there. Your mother can wear me down until I promise anything. She just never has figured out how to get me to keep them.

sunsets

Patterson doesn't stop to see Laney after visiting with his mother. He can't. He knows that if Laney gets him in the same kitchen they used to sit in with Justin she could probably talk him into signing anything. She knows it, too. When Laney knows what she wants, she knows how to get it from him. And she always does if Patterson doesn't plan the occasional strategic absence.

He's driving up the mesa, pulling around the last switchback before the dirt road tops out, when he sees Junior's Charger pulled off by the side of the road. Junior's stretched out on the hood of the car, his hands on his chest, the last of the sunlight scattering across the broken horizon created by the San Juans.

"Visiting Henry?" Patterson asks, stepping out of his truck.

A faint grin plays across Junior's mouth. "You'd be late if I was."

Patterson reaches in his pocket for his cell phone.

"Relax," Junior says. "I'm passing through."

"Passing through?"

"On my way south. El Paso."

"What's in El Paso?"

"The Mexican border. I detour past here when I get sick of I-25." Junior looks sidelong at Patterson. "He's a charmer, but most of the bitches who fall for his shit are broken-down rodeo groupies. You're the first grown man."

"You don't have to work to start a fight with me tonight. You can hop off the hood and I'll kick your ass right here."

Junior chuckles.

"You ain't the only one that's had a rough childhood," Patterson says. "They're writing books about it all the time."

Junior waits a minute. Then, "One of these days, I'm going to lead you right up and introduce you to that old asshole."

"That's what you stopped by here for? To tell me that?"

Junior shakes his head, eyes still closed. "I stopped by here to see the sunset. There ain't a better sunset anywhere in all the world than right here on this mesa."

"And then you're headed to El Paso?"

"El Paso." He opens his eyes as if Patterson had just reminded him that was where he was going. "You want to ride along?"

"Ride along where?"

"El Paso."

Patterson doesn't even think about it. He opens his mouth to say "Hell, no." But just before he can get the words out, his cell phone rings. He pulls it out of his pocket and looks at it. Then stands there for a beat or two holding it in his hand with his thumb ready to answer it while it rings. He slides it, still ringing, back in his pocket. "How long will it take?" Patterson asks. "I gotta be back to work on Monday."

"Shit, we'll be back by noon tomorrow. There's money in it, too. I ain't slept in too goddamn long. I could use somebody to help me stay awake on the drive."

"How much money?"

"Two hundred bucks." Junior grins.

They drive, listening to Brother Joe until they get out of range. The show is about the Branch Davidian raid in Waco. About the FBI and ATF's solution for rumors of child abuse being to pump poison gas into the compound and set all the children on fire. How they claimed not to have fired into the compound at all, even though FLIR footage showed assault rifles and grenade launchers popping off. Brother Joe says that it's the Waco siege that turned him from being a liberal. That he was a good Democrat right up until that day.

"You know what gets me about this shit?" Junior asks, punching the power button on the car radio.

"What shit?"

"Waco. 9/11. All that shit Brother Joe and Henry go on about."

"Tell me."

"People die. All the fucking time, people die. They get blown up, they get set on fire. Shit happens. I've had that goddamn television for about two weeks now and I can't turn it on without seeing some poor son of a bitch getting blown out of his socks."

"It's all reruns," Patterson agrees.

"So how the hell do you pick one set of motherfuckers and decide that's the one you're gonna spend the rest of your life obsessing about? Waco, 9/11, all of that shit, it's ancient history. Find some new shit."

"I think they'd say it's different when it's your own people doing it to you," Patterson answers. "That's what they'd say."

"My people, shit. I don't even know what a Branch Davidian is. They're about just as much my people as the people in the World Trade Center. You know how many Manhattan bankers I've met in my life?" Junior sticks one finger up under his eye patch and rubs. His finger comes out wet. His hand is trembling.

"How's about I drive for a little while?" Patterson asks, wondering exactly how long it has been since he's slept.

"None," Junior continues, ignoring him. "Not fucking one. I got more in common with an Afghani goatherder than I have with a Manhattan banker. I guarantee you that. They just like finding shit to get upset about so's they don't have to worry about their own fucking lives."

"I'm not disagreeing with you."

"I know you aren't. That's why you're up on the mesa drinking yourself stupid. You know just as well as I do that it's all bullshit."

immigrants

It's a storefront bar in El Paso, standing a couple of blocks in the wrong direction from downtown, the name, Green Gables, painted in faded letters beside the barred door. When Patterson and Junior pull up it's opening for breakfast, and a line of old men who'd been sitting along the whitewashed brick wall are filing inside for $2.99 eggs and pork chops. They move in a busted, rubbery shuffle, like they've had most of their bones broken and reset with contact cement. Patterson follows them in and Junior leaves to take care of his business.

It feels good to be somewhere new. Patterson's never made it to El Paso before, and nothing will empty your mind like being somewhere you haven't been. He reads the local newspaper at a table by the door, the June sun rising through the screen door. A dog that looks to be half pit bull comes over from the bar and curls up on the floor beside him. Patterson scratches his neck and misses Sancho while the old men finish their breakfasts and start to drinking beer.

After an hour or so, Patterson folds the paper closed and takes a walk, looking for the Acme Saloon where John Wesley Hardin let himself get killed. That's the only thing he knows about El Paso. Turns out it's a dollar store now, but there's a plaque: *Hardin was shot in the back of the head by El Paso constable John Selman.* Patterson keeps walking. It's boarded-up burger joints and homeless men who've been shrunk down to nothing by drinking in the dust and hot sun. At least until he lucks on Dave's Pawn Shop, where he sees Pancho Villa's trigger finger, a baby vampire's heart, a mummified dog, and a collection of Nazi mother's crosses. He buys an old copy of *Omoo* and returns to the bar to read it.

Lunch comes and goes. There's a dark-skinned woman trying to feed an armless boy, but now and then she forgets what she's doing and gets lost in her tequila glass. So he sits there with his mouth open for so long that his eyes tear up. Patterson watches them until he feels bad. Then he watches them some more. Then he reads.

It's almost three o'clock when Junior returns and sits down at the table. "We've got company coming," he says.

Patterson closes his book, carefully.

"Relax," Junior says. "We'll just have a beer or two. He ain't the kind of person I can say no to."

It occurs to Patterson that there are good choices, there are bad choices, and then there's this one, which isn't even on the map. It's amazing the flat stupidity to which he'll resort when trying to avoid a woman.

"A friend of yours?" he asks.

"You'll love him, he's even crazier'n Henry," Junior says. "And I ain't got a choice."

Patterson stretches and looks around. "I pictured more of the border."

"Trunks open?" Junior says. "Out in the desert somewhere, pulled off Interstate 10 across from the Juárez slums?"

"Maybe Juárez," Patterson says. "Juárez would've been nice."

"Nice, hell. You wouldn't even see it coming in Juárez. El Paso is one of the safest cities in the United States. Juárez is a goddamned slaughterhouse."

"How is El Paso one of the safest cities in the United States and Juárez a slaughterhouse?"

"El Paso's an immigrant city," Junior says. "Immigrant cities are safe."

"But the immigrants are from Juárez, right?"

"Yeah, but Juárez ain't an immigrant city."

Patterson gives up. "So who's your friend?"

"You'll know him when you see him," Junior says.

disneyland

Patterson does know him when he sees him, there's no doubt about it at all. It's sometime around dinner and a construction crew has come in off work. They're pounding pitcher beer and yelling at each other in Spanish when he walks in wearing a Border Patrol polo shirt. Everyone goes suddenly silent as he pulls off his sunglasses and folds them shut, his blond hair swept breezily off his tanned forehead. "Junior," he says, walking to them.

"Carmichael." Junior returns. "This is Patterson."

"Patterson," Carmichael says, and drops into his seat. He's somewhere in his thirties or forties, but his skin is so clear it's hard to tell. He looks like he's spent the better part of his life preserved in Vaseline.

"You really Border Patrol?" Patterson asks. He knows he probably shouldn't be asking questions, but he can't help it.

"Remember the Alamo!" Carmichael yells. Every head in the bar snaps around. He flashes his badge and they all return to what it is they were doing. "I'm fucking with them. I wouldn't bust them on a bet." He sighs happily.

"Isn't that your job?" Patterson asks.

"On the clock." Carmichael shrugs. "These're the only things keeping us free, these places."

"How do you figure?" Patterson asks.

"Think about it," Carmichael says. "You're out on the street, you're on somebody's radar all the time. And you're always breaking the law. You know why?"

"Why?"

"Because there's too many of 'em to even count. There's laws about everything. Smoking. Eating. Mattresses. Even crossing the street. You know how many laws apply to you in Mexico when you need to cross the street?"

"No idea," Patterson says. "I've never been to Mexico."

"None, that's how many. In Mexico, if you need to cross the street, you cross the street. They figure if you're a fully functioning adult you can probably make it across a street without state intervention. That's freedom, son. And it ain't here. Here they've got things like jaywalking ordinances. If you can think of anything more insulting to your freedom I'd like to hear it."

"I've thought about it."

"Think you could name all the laws you're subject to? Right now at this very moment?"

"No," Patterson says. "No idea."

"Fuck no, you can't. Nobody can. You couldn't follow all the laws if you tried. You can take it from me. I can't even name all of them. If somebody wants to put you away, they don't have to invent a reason. They can just scan through the law books, find one or two you're breaking, and there you are, you sorry son of a bitch, you're in jail. Because they're always watching you. You can take that from me."

"They hate us for our freedom. That's what I heard."

"Horseshit," Carmichael says. "That's the thing about Mexicans, we hate them for their freedom. That's what all those peckerwoods down on the border with their rifles and their lawn chairs are protesting. That somebody has the right to just act like they're free. To go wherever they want, freely. Drives them bugshit. I know, I have to deal with them."

"So why is here free?" Patterson asks. "Why this bar? It's in this country, subject to the same laws as everybody else."

"No it ain't." Carmichael shakes his head. "Nobody's watching here. You're invisible. None of these fuckers even exist. They can come and go and nobody even notices. Nobody wants to notice. This country hums along on the simple fact of them not being noticed."

"They're free because they don't exist?"

"Exactly. There's nobody watching them, and when you're in one of their shitholes, there's nobody watching you. With them it's almost like you're living in America."

"You really do love your job." Patterson's a little impressed.

"Fuck yes. I love every one of these little son of a bitches. Those who think they're protecting America by keeping these people out, they're full of shit. There ain't no America left in the places they're protecting. Their fucking malls and their fucking crosswalks and their fucking subdivisions. Freedom's something that's been designed out of those places."

"That's been my general impression of malls," Patterson says.

"That's because you're a thinker. I could tell it by looking at you. Malls are prisons. They are. They're prototypes for the concentration camps. You can believe that. They make it look like they ain't because they control your mind."

Patterson laughs out loud. Now he's truly impressed.

"It's true," Carmichael says. "And you know the worst part?"

"Tell it to me."

"Here it is," Carmichael says. "They're using your own imagination to control it. That way you won't use it yourself to imagine something better." He points at Patterson with his beer. "That's why Disneyland is there, to hide the fact that it's the rest of America that's the real Disneyland. Just like prisons are there to hide the fact that it's the rest of the society that's the real prison. That's a quote."

"You're one of the people building the walls," Patterson says. "It's you, boss."

"True. True." He nods.

"I read somewhere that there are more atheists in the Catholic clergy than anywhere else in America," Patterson continues.

"Also true," he says. Then he says to Junior, "I like this one. You can bring him along anytime."

"Good," Junior says. "And at some point I hope one of you two dipshits will let me in on what the fuck you're talking about."

horse. shit.

It's exactly the night they deserve. They drink beer until Junior gets bored of beer and starts cutting lines of cocaine on the table. There are women, too. Brown-skinned women. Not really flocking to them, but circling Junior, anyway. Patterson starts to wonder about the virtues of an eye patch for himself. Junior, for his part, seems to be ignoring them. Which Patterson is mostly glad of.

"Where are you from?" Carmichael asks Patterson.

"The San Luis Valley," Patterson answers.

"See, I know about the San Luis Valley," Carmichael says. "There are energy vortices in the San Luis Valley."

"There are what?" Patterson says. It's one of the girls distracting him. She's wearing a blue blouse, sloping down over her like a waterfall.

"Energy vortices," Carmichael says. "Why you think there are all those churches? They got Buddhist retreats, Hindu temples, all of it."

"That's being free, too?" Junior says. "Being up on Patterson's mesa?"

"You tell me," Carmichael says. "You're up there nearly as much as he is."

Junior leans forward and snorts a line through a rolled-up five-dollar bill. He straightens, wiping his nose on the back of his hand. "How'd you hear that?" he asks. "About the energy vortices."

"It was on a radio show," Carmichael says. "I used to have to run up to Denver almost as much as you do, at least when I was starting out. And you ain't the only one to get bored with I-25."

"Brother Joe," Junior says. "Please don't tell me it was Brother Joe."

"You've heard it," Carmichael says.

Junior shakes his head and descends for another line. Patterson tries not to watch him too hard. It's nearly impossible. Patterson could use another line himself.

Then Carmichael says, "I met him."

Thoughts of cocaine and brown-skinned girls, they both flee Patterson's head.

"You met who." Junior tosses the rolled-up bill on the bar table. "Who did you meet?"

"Brother Joe," Carmichael says. "I met him."

"Horse. Shit."

"You want to hear the story?"

"Yes," Patterson says. He picks the rolled-up bill off the table, snorts a line. "I most definitely want to hear that story."

mason jars

"**I** was coming back from Denver last fall," Carmichael begins. "It was a weekend trip, and my wife had taken the kids to her parents. I didn't have much to get back to El Paso for, and you know how it is once you start driving up there. So I made it to Fort Garland and decided, fuck it, I'll keep driving. And I did, right through Alamosa, into the Rio Grande National Forest, then up into the San Juan Mountains. I figured I'd find a cabin and rent it for the weekend. It had been a good trip to Denver, but it'd almost gone wrong. I was in need of a little time away.

"But what I didn't count on was how dark it gets up there. That's what got me. There's no kind of cell phone signal, neither, not once you get in the mountains. So I started to get a little weirded out. Which meant I started making turns. Like there has to be a house up here somewhere, right? Somebody I can ask where I can get a room for the night? Then the side roads were dirt, and I was getting really worried now. I couldn't see shit. And I looked down and I only had a quarter tank of gas left.

"That did it. I made it up to the top of this rise, and there was a place to stop, like a pull-off. So I stopped. Fuck it. I can wait until daylight when I can see something, I figured. Try to make my way back then."

"I've been lost up there," Patterson says.

"Not me," says Junior. "I ain't been lost once in my whole life."

"Right," says Carmichael. "So anyway, when I came awake the sun was up. So I looked around, kind of like you will when you wake up in a strange place, trying to figure things out. You know how it is.

"And then I almost shit myself.

"There was somebody standing outside my car. Just the shadow of a man, standing there haloed in the light through the passenger's-side window.

"I sat up, put my hand on my gun, and rolled the window down.

"'This is where I come to watch the sunrise, too,' the man said. He was a big one, wearing a Carhartt jacket with a beard down to the bib of his overalls.

"Well, I hadn't really noticed the sunrise at the time. Just the goddamn sun. So I suppose I blinked around some.

"'Life is a great sunrise,' the man said. 'I do not see why death should not be an even greater one. Nabokov said that.'"

"What book's that from?" Patterson asks.

"You read enough Nabokov to know the difference?" Carmichael asks.

"I read," Patterson says.

"You gotta do something at his age," Junior says.

Carmichael chuckles. "I asked him the same thing. And you know what he said? He said, 'I don't know. I found it on the internet.'

Then he reached in the front pocket of his overalls, took out a bag of tobacco, and began to roll a cigarette. 'Are you lost?'

"'I was trying real hard to be, I guess,' I said. I looked up and down the road. None of it looked even remotely familiar. 'I think I might have made it.'

"'Where are you coming from?'

"'I need to get back to the San Luis Valley. If I can get there, I can figure out the rest.'

"The man shook his head. 'I stay away from the valley,'" he said. "'Too much happens there. Do you know where you are?'

"'I don't have the slightest fucking idea.'

"'You can give me a ride to my house,' the man said. 'I can give you directions.'"

"You saw his house?" Junior says. "Brother Joe's house? Henry'd have an aneurism."

"Who's Henry?"

"He's a fucking groupie, that's what he is," Junior says. "Don't worry about it. Keep going."

"All right." Carmichael nods. "I did see it. And I don't know what I expected. Probably something like a tar-paper shack. Definitely not the log cabin we ended up at. It was beat up, for sure, but it had levels and gables and decks and all kinds of shit. Like one of the McMansions you find down south of Denver, in Castle Rock or Lonetree.

"But when we got out of the car, Jesus. Just at the edge of the stone walkway from the turnaround up to the house's front door there was this heap of something covered by a blue tarp. And the smell coming off it, it was like nothing I ever smelled in my life.

"'It's coyotes,' the man said. 'I cover them up so none of the helicopters that'll fly over will see them. When they stink bad enough that I can smell them in the house, I burn them.'

"'I think you're about there,' I said."

"'We'll see,' he said, and he led me up onto the deck, where there were three mangy dogs sleeping by a porch swing and shriveled rattlesnake skins nailed to the posts. Then he opened the door, and I got exactly what he meant. There were all these Mason jars filled up with all this disgusting shit. Shit that looked like baby thumbs and little fetuses suspended in some kind of fluid. And the lids on the jars were all bulging up like they were gonna blow. I felt my whole body heave.

"It was the most disgusting thing I'd ever seen or smelled, and I've dragged hundreds of dead Mexicans out of the desert. 'Jesus. Holy. Fucking. Christ,' I choked out, doing everything I could not to vomit.

"'Told you that you wouldn't smell the dead ones,' he said. 'That's their anal glands you're smelling now. And vaginas and reproductive organs. Soaking in their own urine.'

"'I got it,' I said. I pulled my shirt up over my nose. 'What in the holy fuck for?'

"'Trapping.' The man nodded at a box of rusty No. 3 traps in the corner of the kitchen. 'You want a drink?'

"'Jesus, yes.'

"'This way.' Now, the living room was lined with books and more animal parts. Shit that I swear to God I ain't never seen walking or flying on this planet. I knew better than to ask, though.

"He pulled off his jacket and tossed it on a chair. He wasn't wearing any kind of shirt under his bib overalls, and he had all these tattoos. Not your normal ones either. Eagles and swastikas and Celtic crosses, all in blue ink. He walked over to a drink cart against one wall and poured us each a glass of bourbon, then sat down in a leather armchair, gesturing me to take the couch.

"'It used to smell worse,' he said. 'For a while I was experimenting with skunk essence and tonquin musk. That was almost unlivable.'

"'I might think about keeping the shit outside,' I said. 'But that's just me.'

"'This is what life is,' he said. 'You gotta let it in.'

"'I'm already neck-deep in anal glands and pussy,' I said. 'Any more might kill me.'

"'You close the doors on the outside world, you close the doors on your soul,' he said.

"I couldn't help it. 'I know who you are,' I said.

"He sat his bourbon glass on an end table and took out this little laptop from somewhere under all the open books and full ashtrays. 'You do?'

"'You're Brother Joe.'

"'You're a listener,' Brother Joe said, opening the laptop.

"'Not regular. Just when I'm driving through.'

"'Half the people who listen to my show say that. They all do a lot of driving.' He pecked at the computer. 'There,' he said. 'Directions to Alamosa, printing.' He pressed another button.

"'Do you believe all that shit?' I asked."

"That's it," Junior says. "That's the question I want to know."

Patterson leans forward. The last time he listened to anything this carefully it was to a doctor.

"Of course I asked it," Carmichael says. "His answer was, 'What shit.'

"'Space platforms,' I said. 'Aliens. The government blew up the World Trade Center. All that shit.'

"'See all those?' Brother Joe waved his hand around at the books.

"I see them.

"'There's more. I have a whole basement full of them.' He chucked his head at a door. 'In there's my study. And in my study are two robotic backup tape libraries, each of which holds thirty terabytes of data. They're almost full with pictures, video, books. Even the largest book is no larger than a megabyte, and each terabyte is one million megabytes. You follow me?'

"'Not in the slightest.'

"He nodded. 'There's too much information in this house, this house alone, to believe anything. I don't believe, I assemble. And what I assemble is what you hear on my show.'

"'So you don't believe any of it?'

"He pulled on his beard, and then smiled. 'Are there nights I can't sleep? There are nights I'm so fucking scared I can't breathe.'

"'So you believe it.'

"'Let's try this," he said. 'You ever heard of Seven World Trade Center?'

"'Sure. It's the building y'all say is proof of a controlled demolition.'

"'Exactly,' he said. 'One of those terabytes of data in that room consists of video, pictures, and reports that prove it was exactly that, a controlled demolition. Another terabyte consists of video, pictures, and reports proving that it was not.'

"'And which do you believe?'

"He laughed out loud. 'Have you ever tried to absorb one terabyte of data? To hold it in your head at one time, let alone weigh it against another?'

"'Other people do. That's how they write those reports.'

"'They foreclose on new information. They make a guess, and call it final.' He got up and walked into the study. When he came back, he handed me directions back to Alamosa. 'Remember,' he said. 'These directions are for planning your route only. Conditions may differ from what's shown on the map.'"

cops

"That's it?" Junior asks. "That's the whole fucking story?"

Carmichael shrugs. "That's the whole story."

Junior shakes his head. "I listened to that whole fucking thing and that was it," he says to himself.

"What about the tattoos?" Patterson asks. "You remember anything specific about them? Those mean something. More so if he's going to put them on his body."

"I don't remember anything specific," Carmichael says. "The swastikas threw me. All's I remember besides them are the eagles and weird Celtic shit."

"You're like a bitch, Patterson," Junior says. "You gotta find something that's got to do with you in every story."

"Could you get back there?" Patterson asks Carmichael. "Son of a bitch," he says, in awe of his own idea.

"Not a chance," Carmichael says. "I mean I could if I had those directions he printed me, but those are long gone."

"Well, I'm fucking disgusted," Junior says. "Most pointless story I ever heard. Except for that line about being neck-deep in anal glands. That was quality." He looks around the bar. "She's gonna have to make it up to me," he says. It's the girl in the blue blouse he's talking about.

Carmichael's leaning back in his chair, one foot up on the chair across from him. Patterson can tell that he's had enough of playing second to Junior, especially in the eyes of the brown-skinned girls. "What's it look like under there?" he asks Junior.

"What's what look like?"

"Under there." Carmichael points at Junior's bad eye. "Under the patch."

Junior's good eye looks at him in a way that Patterson's seen before. The clip knife Junior's using to chop his cocaine has a drop-point blade that comes in over three inches, and Patterson knows that he's also carrying his Glock. "What do you see?" Junior asks. He waves the knife in a circle toward Carmichael's face. "Under there."

Carmichael tilts his head. "Not sure I follow you, son."

"No," Junior says. "I'm not sure you do." That girl in the blue blouse, she's circled back near them. Her face is so impenetrably young that Patterson looks at his feet. "Come here," Junior says to her. But as she's making her way to the table, he tries to throw his foot up on the chair across from him like Carmichael, and spills sideways out of his chair. "Goddamn it," he mutters.

Carmichael pounds the table, laughing.

"Goddamn it," Junior says again. He rights himself in his chair. Then he looks down at the small pile of cocaine in front of him. "That's all that's left," he says, very, very sadly.

. . .

It's exactly the night they deserve. And as Carmichael has been saying all night, being Anglo in a Mexican bar means never having to say you're sorry. And so, Carmichael suggests they take a walk. He leads them a couple of blocks over to another saloon, this one with no sign at all, just a peeling red storefront and a heavy steel door through which they can hear the sounds of pool balls clicking.

"Stay here," Carmichael says, and he leaves Junior and Patterson to wait on the sidewalk. The night runs low and hot and dark, eddying around them. With the cocaine running out of his system, Patterson's starting to have doubts about the wisdom of this trip again. These are doubts he'll have several more times.

Then Carmichael's back, behind some teenage Mexican boy he shoves out through the bar door and sends crashing to his knees on the sidewalk with a hard kidney punch.

"Who the hell's he?" Patterson says. But Junior reaches over and slaps him on the chest, shakes his head not to say anything more.

"I got nothing for you," the boy says in flawless English to Carmichael. He spits blood and tries to stand upright, his legs wobbling rubberlike under him. Carmichael wipes a loose lock of hair out of his eyes, grabs the front of the boy's shirt, and drags him around the corner of the bar.

Patterson watches the corner wall. Thinks that he needs to go around that corner. That whatever's happening back there is something he needs to stop.

"Don't even think about it, partner," Junior says.

Then it's over, and Carmichael returns holding a baggie of cocaine in his teeth and wiping blood off his arms and hands with the kid's white T-shirt. He wads it up into a ball and tosses it in the gutter.

• • •

Inside another bar there's nobody but a fat lady bartender and a dog. There seems to be a dog in every bar. "Ain't you got any girls?" Carmichael asks the bartender.

She shakes her head. "Cops," she says. "They took all the girls. The local business owners, they want to clean up the area. You want girls, you go to Juárez."

"Cops," Carmichael repeats with some disgust. He digs the coke out of his pocket and tosses it on the table.

"That's what they call being hoisted by your own petard, partner," Junior says.

"Cut yourself a line," Carmichael says. "One big enough to shut your fucking mouth."

Junior does. But when he raises up off the line, he keeps sniffing, like he's trying to snort the oxygen out of the air. "Goddamn it," he says. His voice is thick and hoarse. He pulls up his boot and looks at the sole.

"What is it?" Patterson asks.

"Dog shit. I knew I been smelling it."

"Probably that goddamn mutt right there," Carmichael says.

Junior stands. The bartender is out of sight, in the back somewhere. Junior walks over to where the dog is sleeping under a bar stool, and very carefully, so as not to wake it, he moves the bar stool away. Then he kicks the animal in the ribs so hard that it lifts off the ground and slams into the bar. He rears back and kicks it again, then pulls his gun.

Carmichael throws his arm around Junior's neck and Patterson grabs his gun hand, and the three of them fall together on the floor. The dog stays where it is, twitching and whining. Then it begins to puke blood in frothing waves. Patterson gets the gun out of Junior's hand. He sees himself jamming the muzzle into Junior's forehead and shooting him. He throws the gun off to the side before he does it.

"You bastards," the fat lady says, looking over the bar at them. "You get the fuck out of here."

"Watch your mouth, bitch," Carmichael says to her, standing.

"No." She's crying now. Big tears squeezing out of the corners of her eyes. "You get out of here. I don't care who you are."

truth or
consequences

They drive out of El Paso well before dawn. Patterson doesn't think Junior can even talk. He'll start to, but then he shuts down before he can get the first word out. Patterson can see him trying to make some kind of explanation of himself, but it's like there are two of him. The first flesh and bone, a twitching mass of impulses spilling out all over the place, and the second some terrorist that sits in perpetual judgment on the first. There's times, watching him, when Patterson half expects him to pull out his gun, stick it to his temple, and pull the trigger right there. Just to make it clear who he is.

They stop for food at an all-night diner in Truth or Consequences, New Mexico. They don't speak except for ordering. Patterson's old enough that when the cocaine runs out of his system it takes most of his brains with it. But then the coffee comes, and, after a cup, he gives it a try. "It's a hell of a name," he says over a plate of huevos rancheros. "Truth or Consequences."

"Sounds biblical, don't it?" says Junior. His face looks like he's just washed it in gasoline. Blotchy and swollen. Rubbed raw here, oily there.

"Sounds biblical all right. Sounds fucking terrifying."

"It was named after a radio quiz show," Junior says. "The host said he'd air it from the first American city to name itself after the show. This is the first one that bit."

"Exactly how many times have you driven this route?"

Junior points with his butter knife at a family a couple of tables over. "See them?" It's a man, a woman, and a teenage girl. The man's jaw extends a half foot below his mouth and the woman is no less horse-faced, both of them with brown hair that sticks up here and there like straw in the mud. The girl is fifteen or sixteen, towheaded, with small, furtive features.

"I see them," Patterson says.

"What's the girl look like to you?"

Patterson squints at them, trying to see whatever it is that Junior sees. "Like a girl that's tired of traveling? Like she's sick of her family?"

"Think she looks like them? Like the couple?"

"She's missing the lantern jaw?" Patterson tries.

"That's what I think," Junior says.

"What's what you think?"

"That she doesn't look like them."

"Well," Patterson says. "I'm glad we got that settled."

Junior drops his knife and fork clattering on his plate and signals the waitress for the check.

Patterson stands, banging the table with his knee. "I'm gonna have to go puke before we leave," he says.

"Get on it, partner."

• • •

Patterson wakes to the sound of Junior's car door slamming shut. His eyes jolt open fast, too fast, spots of light and dark flickering across his vision. Junior's moving around the car to the trunk. Patterson runs his hand down his face to make sure everything's in place, then looks around. Rest stop by the highway, the sun rising. He must've fallen asleep while Junior drove.

Then he catches a glimpse of Junior, and where he's heading. "Oh shit." He hits the door handle, spilling out onto the blacktop just as Junior swings his tire iron into the driver's window of a fifteen-year-old Ford station wagon three spaces down. The window shatters and the lantern-jawed redneck raises his arms to protect himself. Junior swings through his arms, the end of the tire iron smashing into the redneck's forehead.

The horse-faced woman hurtles around the hood, waving a hawksbill knife, her eyes straining out of her skull. Patterson's on his feet, running. He slams his fist square into her face, the blow jamming his knuckles up into his elbow. She drops in a heap at tire level and she doesn't move anymore, not even a little.

"Get the girl out of there," Junior growls. He reaches through the smashed window, pops the door open, and drags the motionless redneck free of the car, onto the blacktop, raising the tire iron again.

The girl is huddled on the floorboards, hissing at Patterson through her teeth. Patterson opens the door and, dodging her nails, pulls her out of the car by the arm.

cauliflower

She's pissed herself sometime during the attack, so they pull off at an interstate Walmart. Junior parks back in the lot, by the semitrucks and RVs. Patterson is holding his punching hand in his lap. It's swollen up like a cape cauliflower.

"That's why I used the tire iron," Junior says, turning the car off. "I don't punch hardheaded rednecks in the face with my hand. Might as well go around punching salt blocks."

"You were better prepared than I was," Patterson says. He can no longer feel his fingers at all. His hand is a kind of throbbing club, the skin pulling, straining. "I feel like the fucking thing's going to fall off."

Junior turns his head toward the backseat. "You awake?"

"I'm awake," she answers.

"We're at Walmart. You got any money?"

She shakes her head in the rearview mirror. Her fine blond hair moves like mist with her face.

"I'm going to go get you some clothes and some kind of traveling kit," Junior says. "Toothbrush, soap, that kind of shit?"

"Thanks," she says in a low voice.

Junior nods for a second or two. Then he exits the car and walks toward the Walmart.

Patterson opens his door. "Fresh air," he says thickly. She follows him, climbing out of the car between the backseat and the doorframe. Patterson leans against the side of the car, being careful not to accidentally look at his hand. They're quiet for a few minutes. Smoking, watching cars pull in and out. Patterson's hand is running wet with the pain like it's bleeding. Patterson doesn't let it trick him into looking at it. "Where are you from?" he asked her finally.

"San Antonio," she says.

"We're not kidnapping you."

"Okay."

Then he has to be quiet again and work on not vomiting, the thing on the end of his arm throbbing.

Junior finally comes out of the store. He has three plastic shopping bags slung around one hand, a cigarette in the other. "Change in the car," he says to the girl, tossing the bags on the hood. She takes them and crawls into the backseat. Junior slaps the door shut after her. "Where's she from?" he asks.

"San Antonio," Patterson says.

He thinks for a minute. "We can't drive her all the way to San Antonio."

"Well. We can't leave her here."

The door opened and she climbs out of the car wearing cheap jeans, a One Direction T-shirt, and a pair of white tennis shoes. "Who were those assholes?" Junior asks her.

"They picked me up hitchhiking."

"How long have they had you?"

"Since last night."

"You need to go to the hospital?"

"They didn't have time," she says. "They drove all night, scared the police was going to get them."

"All right," says Junior.

"They didn't," she says again.

"All right," says Junior. "We're trying to figure out what to do with you."

"You don't have to do anything with me. You can leave me right here."

"How's about if we take you to the next bus station? Buy you a ticket to San Antonio?"

"You can take me to the bus station," she says.

"But you ain't going back to San Antonio," Junior says.

"Never." She shakes her head. Her eyes redden and her chin trembles. "Fuck him."

Junior presses his bad eye into his shoulder. His eye patch having disappeared sometime during the night, there's no telling where. "You got anywhere to go at all?"

"I got a cousin in Casper," she says.

Justin

I don't know how Junior knew what was happening. I'm not sure Junior even knows how Junior knew what was happening. Or if he even knew anything was really happening at all. It could be that he just needed something to recover him from our night in El Paso, and that was the first thing he spotted. That he just got lucky and there really was somebody who needed helping.

But that's not what's eating me up. It's that there are men who would do that to children. To their own children. There's times I don't sleep for three or four nights. It's like somebody stuffed a rag down my throat and parked a truck on my chest. I can't think about anything else but sitting in the hospital with you. Or about him, Dr. Court. I go whole nights sitting awake thinking about beating him to death with my own hands. There's nothing I wouldn't do to bring you back.

And then there's his kind. Who'd run off his own daughter. Who probably raped her or beat her, but who definitely, and worse than anything else he ever could have done, abandoned her. Who left her out there alone, easy pickings for any psychopath on the road. To starve, die, or smash herself against his absence for the rest of her life.

They put people in prison for taking drugs. They lock kids away for stealing money from gas stations, for joyriding in cars. But men who abandon their children, they float through life, as light as air.

more

Junior cuts the engine in front of his house. Then he has to sit for a while, staring at his lap with his arms draped over the steering wheel. He feels like the world's driving out from under him. Maybe Jenny's got the right idea. Maybe he just needs to get the fuck out of Denver. Not Highlands Ranch, no way he could do that, but maybe Greeley. Get his CDL and drive a truck or something.

Then he raises his head and sees the man sitting on his stoop. The sheer size of him, somewhere between a bear and a mountain. When Eduardo's not sitting next to the much smaller Vicente it's not quite as striking how big he is. But it's still enough to take your breath away.

Junior knows the day's not yet done.

"A rough run?" Eduardo asks when Junior gets out of the car. Even the ruin that is his face is the size of Junior's chest.

Junior eases himself down next to him on the cement stoop. "I was going to get cleaned up before I made the drop."

"That is a good idea," Eduardo says. "Vicente would worry if he saw you like this. He would think you had been in a fight."

Junior looks down at his battered hands. And the dog blood and filth covering his clothes. "Not really."

"Not really, like you weren't in a fight?"

"Not really, like there wasn't much fight to it."

"Ah," Eduardo says. He's wearing a leather vest. He reaches into an inside pocket and pulls out a cigar, his brown arms tattooed so thickly and long ago it looks like a pattern of intricate bruising. "Do you mind if I smoke?"

"Knock yourself out," Junior says.

"I was hoping to talk to you alone." Eduardo incinerates the end of the cigar with a lighter that looks like a small jet engine. "Vicente is already worried about you," he says. "More worried than he will show to me. Which means that I should be even more worried than he is. For him."

"Ain't a thing in the world to worry about me for," Junior says.

"Is it the cocaine?" Eduardo asks. "Is that the problem?"

"No," Junior says. "That ain't the problem."

"We can get you treatment if cocaine is the problem," Eduardo says. "If cocaine is the problem it will be hard work for you, but there is help, and we will get it for you."

"Cocaine ain't the problem."

"Well, then," Eduardo says. He blows a stream of cigar smoke at the leaves of the cottonwood in front of Junior's house. "What is?"

"Life, maybe," Junior says. "Hell, I don't know."

"It's hard to be young," Eduardo says.

"Life's a shit sandwich and sooner or later everybody takes a bite," Junior says. "That's how I'd put it."

"Have you read that book?" Eduardo asks. "The one I gave you? *Brave of Heart*?"

Junior nods. "Just finished it."

"There is some help in that book," Eduardo says. "There is a reason La Familia uses it."

"I thought the book was gibberish. Isn't that what you said?"

Eduardo shakes his head. "Vicente said that. Vicente is quick to dismiss things."

"But not you?"

"Not me. A man does need more. He needs a greater orbit than exists for him. He needs a life worthy of his heart. Of God's heart. He needs a war, a crusade, a maiden to rescue." Eduardo looks up and down the street. "If this was my life, the only life I had to live, I would choose not to live it. The life of the people in these houses. Useless work and more useless wives. That is no life."

"That ain't what my old lady's telling me," Junior says. "She's telling me that the key to my life is to get me into a real job, not out of one. She's of the opinion that drug running ain't the best of all possible life choices."

Eduardo reaches behind his head and adjusts his ponytail. Then he looks for a second or two too long at Junior. "It's not the drug running. It's the decisions you make and the things in your head. Decisions and thoughts worthy of a man, that's what you need."

"In fact, I done the rescuing of a maiden lately," Junior says. "And if you know where the war is, you just point me at the motherfucker."

"I cannot do that for you," Eduardo says. "It's your battle." He claps his huge hand on Junior's shoulder. "Another thing."

"Go ahead."

"Somebody else has been looking for your friend."

Junior feels his whole body go tight. "What friend?"

"The gringo alcoholic."

"Yeah, who?"

"It is a woman," Eduardo says. "A woman with black hair."

Junior laughs.

Eduardo looks at Junior for a long time. His eyes are black and limpid.

"Right," Junior says.

"This woman is the head of a biker gang that runs most of the meth in St. Louis," Eduardo says. "That is what she does."

"Right," Junior says again.

Eduardo squeezes his arm. "You cannot afford friends who attract this kind of attention. Even if they do not know what it is that you do. I know that you would not be stupid enough to expose yourself, but you cannot afford friends who expose you. And this friend of yours, that is what he does. He exposes people. He endangers people."

"I understand," Junior says.

"Good." Eduardo stands. He stretches, his arms spanning horizon to horizon. "Read the book," he says. "Try to think clear, straight thoughts, and read the book. It will help."

progress

Patterson wakes up bundled up on the couch, a bandage on his hand and his nose taped up. Sancho is curled up on his legs, looking at him balefully. Worse, Laney is sitting at the table, drinking a cup of coffee and reading a book, Gabe next to her drawing something in a coloring book. Patterson opens his mouth to speak, but nothing comes out. He clears his throat, drags up a mouse-sized hunk of mucus, and swallows it. The room swims in a nauseous yellow cloud. He gags.

"Hello," Laney says. "How are you feeling?"

"I'm all right," Patterson says.

"No," she says. She holds her slightly red nose over her cup of coffee and inhales. "You're not all right."

"I'm not?"

"Do you remember the hospital?" she asks.

He shakes his head.

"You have two hairline fractures, a pulled muscle, and your wrist is sprained. I didn't even know you could sprain a wrist, but you did it. You also have a broken nose, apparently from falling face-first into the floor about two steps after you made it into the cabin. And there was some talk about the amount of cocaine and alcohol in your system, both in quantities that probably should have killed you."

"It felt worse," Patterson says.

"Exhaustion, too, but Henry, Emma, and I had stopped listening at that point. That was who found you, by the way. Henry and Emma. If it wasn't for them, you'd still be lying on your floor."

"I was pretty tired," Patterson agrees.

"Also," she continues, "there was blood on you that the doctor said came from different sources. And at different times. Some on the cuffs of your pants and your shoes, and some more on your shirt."

Patterson nods. "What was on my pants and shoes was dog's blood. Most of it probably dog vomit, actually."

"Good. That clears that up."

"You're being sarcastic."

"Yes, I am. Is it safe to say that if the blood on your pants is from a dog, then the blood on your shirt isn't?"

"That's safe to say."

"So the blood on your shirt, who is that from?"

"I didn't catch her name."

"Her?"

"She was a pedophile."

"Good," she says again. "As long as she deserved it."

"You're being sarcastic again."

"Yes, I am. Do you think you'll be seeing your friend again?

Henry's son? Or do you think maybe Henry might have a point about his character?"

Patterson thinks about Henry. And about Junior. And about the girl on the road. "I don't know," he says.

"That's progress," she says. "I don't know is actually great progress. I'm not trying to nag you. But I really, really, really do think that Junior might not be the best influence on you."

scientists

The doctor from the hospital has written him a prescription for Vicodin, so Patterson eats pills by the fistful, pounding himself into a haze until his hand starts to look like a hand again. Vicodin's something he got pretty well acquainted with from the time shortly after Justin died. The thing about grieving is how much you need to just sit still and stare, how little you need to try to figure things out. That's what's always made him like pills. It makes it easier to sit still and stare at things without trying to make sense of them.

Laney takes care of him while he recuperates from the El Paso trip. She cooks meals, cleans the cabin, feeds Sancho. She talks to him about books she's reading, and even borrows Henry's generator and television so he can watch Westerns. And she doesn't once mention anything about a lawsuit or signing papers. She seems to understand how poorly that kind of talk is working out for Patterson.

Henry stops by on the third night of his recuperation. "How you doing, Patterson?" he asks, standing in the doorway.

"I'm good." Patterson's eating an apple and reading some of what he'd written leading up to his trip to El Paso, trying to figure out what the hell he'd been thinking. "I hear I owe you a thank-you."

"You'd do the same for me if you found me half-dead and full of cocaine." He still hasn't entered the cabin. "I take it he's not doing any better for himself?"

"He's doing what he can," Patterson says.

"Where's Laney?"

"She's got Gabe out in the outhouse."

Henry walks a few steps in and knocks the door shut with his cane.

"Did I do something to piss you off?" Patterson asks.

"No." He pinches his nose between his thumb and forefinger. "Actually, yeah," he says. "Paulson's fit to be tied."

"I figured he fired me."

"He would have. I told him your mother died."

"Thanks."

"Fuck you."

The door opens and Laney walks in, holding Gabe's hand. "Are you fighting?" she asks.

"I don't fight with drunks," says Henry. "Nor druggies."

Patterson grins genially. He's having an easy time being genial with all the Vicodin floating through his system.

"Are you ready?" Henry asks Laney.

"Where are y'all headed?" Patterson asks.

"Henry bought a telescope," Laney says. "He's got it set up on the roof of the barn, and there's supposed to be a meteor shower tonight. He thought we might want to see it."

"Not a shower," Henry says. "Some activity."

"It'd do you good for you to get out of the house," Laney says. "I was hoping we could talk you into it."

"I'll sit here and thank my own stars, instead," Patterson says. "Thank them for having the kind of friend who'll lie to my boss for me. But y'all should go."

"Wouldn't hurt you to see a star or two you didn't make up," Henry says.

"Sure," Patterson says. "When'd you get interested in astronomy?"

"Thus is the excellence of God magnified and the greatness of His kingdom made manifest," Henry quotes. "He is glorified not in one, but in countless suns. Not in a single earth, a single world, but in a thousand thousand."

"Well," Patterson says. "Good luck."

"Patterson's morally opposed to any attempt to make meaning out of the world," Henry explains to Laney. "If he was a serial killer he'd kill priests and scientists."

"Not only priests and scientists," Patterson corrects him. "Mostly priests and scientists."

"It's also why he never talks about politics," Henry continues. "He doesn't like to make sense out of anything."

"Can we talk about something else?" Even as genial as the Vicodin is making Patterson, he's done with this conversation.

Henry looks at him for a long time. "Another thing about you."

"Don't bother."

"No, one more thing. Junior."

"Not Junior," Laney says. "Definitely not Junior."

"Hold on," Henry says to her. "This is what I'm getting at. Patterson and Junior, they're circling. You know why?"

"No," says Laney. "I don't know why."

"They're two of a kind," Henry says. "Junior, he can't stand to make sense out of anything either. He's another like Patterson. He can't stand to believe in nothing."

"Horseshit," Patterson says. "He believes in you. And look at all the good it's doing him."

rope

After they leave, Patterson realizes Laney is right, he does need to get out of the cabin. So he belts on his .45 and goes for a walk. The stars are thrown over the matte black sky like pebbles strewn across a creek bed, and seeing the night overhead makes him think a little clearer. He's not sure what good it does, but when he gets back to the cabin he pours a drink and stretches out on the couch with a book. Thinking is good, but reading is good protection against thinking too much. As is drinking. Patterson gets the feeling he's living out a kind of exercise to see which slips under his guard first.

They don't bother knocking. The man swings the door open and sweeps inside, his movements clean and practiced. He's taller than Patterson, gaunt, with long, gray-black hair that runs right down into his beard. There's a tattoo on his arm of a winged skull and the words *Semper Fi*, and he's holding a very mean-looking AR-15 on a single-point sling on his chest. Patterson's known plenty of his kind on work crews. Ruined by whichever Gulf War they were in, renting themselves out for muscle work wherever they can find it.

And the woman who follows the biker through the door, Patterson recognizes her immediately. Adrenaline hits him like a bucket of cold water, blood rushing into his ears like a dam bursting. He lays his book on the floor, carefully. "You gotta be fucking kidding me," he says to her, his voice smearing in his ears.

"Where's the dog?" the man asks. Patterson's heard chain saws with more human feeling than his voice.

"He's out. He stays out most nights. I can go three or four without seeing him." Patterson speaks slowly, thinking his way through the words, letting his body recover from the shock.

"Stand up," the man says. "And keep your hands where I can see them."

Patterson swings his feet off the couch and places his glass on the floor. He wills his hand not to shake, but it doesn't do him much good. Then he puts his hands out at the man, showing there's nothing in them. "You mind closing the door before the mosquitoes get in?"

The man doesn't give any indication that he's heard Patterson at all. He stands by the open door, his left hand resting on the AR-15's grip, not even bothering to point it at him. "All right," Patterson says. "We can sort this out." He tries to look as scared as he can. It doesn't take a whole hell of a lot of effort. "Close the door and I'll tell you whatever you want to know."

"That's why we're here," Mel says. "I need you to tell me where Chase is."

Patterson doesn't even bother thinking about cover. There's nowhere in the cabin the biker can't shoot him as easy as if he were standing a foot in front him. He knows that as well as Patterson does, which is why he isn't bothering to put his sights on him. "Jesus, you're a badass," Patterson says. "You do remember that I untied you out of that bathtub?"

Her eyes don't waver.

"He didn't mean you any good," Patterson says. "In case you hadn't figured that out."

"Where is he?" she says.

Patterson knows there isn't a lie in the world he can come up with that would satisfy her. So he does what he seems to do best. Plays stupid. "What makes you think I know?"

"He came down here looking for you," she says.

"He did," Patterson says. "And I told him I didn't have you. Nor his dope, which is what he was really after."

"Shut your mouth," she says.

"This make a goddamn bit of sense to you?" Patterson asks the biker.

The man doesn't answer and his gun hand doesn't move, but Patterson thinks he sees something happen around his eyes.

Patterson tries a different tack. "I've got people who'll be back any minute," he says.

"We brought rope," she says. "We're not staying."

"They'll figure it out," Patterson says. "Everybody knows everybody up here on the mesa, somebody'll see your car."

"Get your shoes on," she says. "And we'll give it a try."

"Jesus," Patterson says. "Over a fuckup like Chase."

"Put your shoes on."

"Okay," Patterson says. "Okay. Close the door."

This time the command seems to click in the biker's head. Without even thinking, he reaches out with his gun hand and slaps the door shut.

As soon as his hand hits the door, Patterson sweeps back, pulls his .45 one-handed, and punches the pistol at the man's chest, squeezing the trigger twice. The two-shot string is one solid boom like somebody set off a stick of dynamite between his eyes. It's point shooting at that range, and Patterson's scared he missed at first. Until the biker looks down at his chest, startled, and slumps to the floor.

Mel's moving. "Don't," Patterson yells to her. He can't hear himself over the sound of his eardrums splintering. He doubts she can either. She's squatted down by the man, tugging at the AR-15. She probably thinks she's moving quickly, and maybe she is, but to Patterson it's all comically slow. She struggles with the sling, looking for a way to unfasten it.

"Don't," Patterson tries again, louder.

She gets the AR-15 loose, and that's all the time Patterson can give her. He jerks the trigger and the bullet goes through her arm, blows into her chest cavity. Her eyes widen and the breath goes out of her as her legs give. She very slowly, almost graciously, collapses forward across the biker.

Patterson breathes out. "You bitch," he says. And he sits down at the table and stares at the two bodies.

dirt

Patterson doesn't know how long he sits at the kitchen table. This is as close as he's ever come to being killed, and he knows it. Mel's face had made that clear, and the biker had been as smooth a professional as Patterson's ever seen. Patterson knows he only survived by dumb luck. Dumb luck and spending way too much time working on his draw.

It probably isn't five minutes he sits there, but it feels like hours. And he's not sure what he's waiting for. Maybe somebody to show up, maybe a police siren. But then he starts to realize that nobody's coming. That unless somebody happened to be walking along the road right then, nobody could've heard the shots. And he also realizes that the last thing he wants to do is explain any of this to Laney, Gabe, and Henry. Let alone the police. So he bubbles his bottle of Evan Williams and chases the whiskey with Vicodin. He needs all the nerve he can get.

Moving fast, holding his breath that they don't come through the door, he has the bodies wrapped in tarps and bound with duct tape within fifteen minutes. There isn't much blood. A trickling, most of it absorbed by their clothes. As advertised, none of the hollow point rounds exited their bodies. In fifteen minutes more, he has his floor scrubbed down and rescuffed with San Luis Valley dirt.

Then he steps outside and sees their car around the corner. It's a Corvette ZR1. Atomic orange, spotless down to its slick black tires, no more than a year old. Patterson's never seen a ZR1 except in pictures in car magazines, and even with two bodies in his living room he can't help but gawk a little as he realizes it's his, at least for the night.

But he doesn't gawk long before he's back inside to get the bodies. Somehow he gets Mel's folded into the trunk. The biker he has to kick into place in the passenger's seat. He tosses a shovel and a bag of lime after them, and peels out down the mesa, toward Questa on CO-159.

It's the opposite of how he felt when he found Chase's body. He doesn't feel bad at all. He feels better than he has in years. To have somebody show up at your house with a gun, to try to kill you, and then win out. Patterson doesn't feel guilty or complicated or even sad. For the first time in a long time, he feels like he's done exactly the right and necessary thing.

He turns on the radio and spins the dial slowly, leaning into it like a sonar operator plumbing the deep, short bursts of static flickering across the airwaves in the big radio-dead valley. Then he comes across Brother Joe. Knowing better, he keeps spinning the dial. Lucks on Willie Nelson singing "He Was a Friend of Mine" and leaves it right there. Which is probably a mistake, the way country music seeps into everything. But he does it anyway.

He crosses the New Mexico line and makes random turns toward the mountains. Off the blacktop and onto the dirt roads, anything he figures the undercarriage can handle, right up to an overgrown four-wheeling trail. Patterson drives it as far as he can with the lights off, and when it gets rough enough he can't drive any farther, he parks and checks the time on his cell phone. Eleven fifteen.

He digs a four-foot-deep hole and rolls the bodies into it. And it breaks his heart, but he tosses the AR-15 in with them. Then he climbs down, slices the tarps with his clip knife, and empties the bag of lime over them. He's a lot smarter this second time around.

pop

Two o'clock in the morning, and Junior has no idea why he's sitting in his car parked down the street from Jenny's house. Especially since his own house is right there. But it is what he's doing. And he's been resisting the urge to go over and tap on her window. To sneak inside and crawl into her bed. To look in on Casey, to just sit and watch her, to put his hand on her forehead, on her cheek.

Junior remembers his own mother waking him with that gesture when he was a boy, and at about the same time in the morning. A hand on the forehead, then on the cheek, as if checking him for a fever. Which she may have been, given that he'd been with Henry while she was working second shift, waiting tables at an all-you-can-eat pancake house.

They'd lived in a double-wide outside of Longmont, Colorado, with room for a horse, though Junior doesn't remember Henry ever actually being able to afford a horse. Most nights when Junior's mother was at work, he and Henry would go down to the only bar in walking distance.

There was barely room for fifty people in that bar, but that was never a problem. There were seldom more than ten at any one time, and most of them broken-down rodeo bums. There was a bartender, though, a redheaded girl in her early twenties, who would spend her nights standing at the end of the bar with Henry. Or, when she got a chance, and there was no one else in the place but she and Henry and Junior, would lock the front door and sneak back to the stockroom with him.

Junior tried not to notice it when they snuck off together. That was one of many betrayals of his mother. He loved that place, and he wasn't about to fuck that up. There was a television, which they didn't have the money for at their trailer, and when business was slow, the redhead would open up the pinball machine and let him play for free. And when the boy was tired, Henry'd make him a bed along the seat of one of the three booths that were used for weekly euchre games by a gang of half-crippled rough-stock riders.

Then there was Henry himself. The broken places hadn't yet hardened, and he moved with a loose, looping grace that he wore as easily as his friendship. He was almost impossible not to love when he wasn't at home, and here, in the bar, he was at his best. He let the boy steer the conversation, let him wander as far off topic as he wanted. Never pushing him in any direction, just rolling along on Junior's trip. Joking and laughing, doing what he did that made him popular in every bar he'd ever set foot in, and bringing Junior into his world.

Most nights, after the smoke and the boozy talk and the television, the last thing Junior remembered was curling up exhausted in the booth, letting himself drift away on the warm tones of Henry's voice. And then partially wakening as Henry picked him up and carried him all the way back to their trailer, where he tucked him into bed. And, later, waking again, for just a minute, as his mother put her hand on his forehead, on his cheek.

Only to come awake one more time to the sound of yelling, Henry and Connie hard after each other again.

And then, and Junior's never quite sure of this memory, he was standing against the fence out back of their trailer, not much more than eight years old. One of Henry's rodeo buddies was standing next to him, a sharp-faced man with a long, scraggly mustache. Neither of them talking, just watching what was happening on the other side of the fence about fifty feet away, watching as Henry dragged Connie backward by the hair. She was screaming and scratching over her head at his hands and arms, her legs scrabbling to keep up.

"Don't you think we ought to do something?" Junior remembers asking. He looked at his father's friend, who was smoking a lumpy hand-rolled cigarette.

"I ain't getting in the middle of that," the man said. He looked at the boy. "I got some pop in my truck. How's about you and me go get one?"

Henry let go of Connie's hair, and she fell flat on her back. He stood over her, looking down, his chin jutted out like a rooster's. Then he turned and strutted toward the fence. He only made it four or five paces before she rose behind him and charged in a low, crablike run, her mane of dirty blond hair tangled with dry grass and clumps of dirt. She was fully airborne when she hit his back, and they dropped together, rolling through the tall grass in a flurry of blows and dust, screaming and hissing. And then the motion quieted, and there were only Henry's grunts, and the solid smack of blows landing on undefended flesh.

"I think we'd better go get that pop," Henry's friend said.

Connie was in the hospital for two days, and it was another week before she could work again. She and Henry spent her time off in the kitchen, drinking black coffee and talking. They kept the shades drawn and the trailer was heavy and dark. They were pounding out some kind of deadly agreement that Junior neither understood nor cared to. Junior, out of school for the summer, listened to the radio and read comic books in his room. He hated both of them desperately. And when she finally did go back to work, Junior no longer went with Henry to the bar.

Most of the memories that gnaw at the edges of Junior's brain are like that. They come in fragments. A conspiracy of whispered voices, crashes in the bedroom, pus and blood draining from his mother's swollen eye the next morning. Henry sitting on the front step of the trailer, waiting for Junior to walk down the lane from school. Grabbing the boy into his arms, crying drunk into his neck.

And then there was when she died. And that, too, was the old man's doing somehow, if for no other reason than it was her dying that stopped him from drinking. Junior knows that Henry's sobriety was an acknowledgment of his complicity in her death, just as he knows that the minute Henry got sober, his mother's death became just one more point in Henry's story of Henry.

And Junior knows himself for what he is in Henry's life. A terrorist, forcing himself into Henry's story of himself, making himself relevant in something in which he has always been irrelevant. Henry's story of himself is total, self-configuring, and self-healing. There is nothing that cannot be assimilated by it. Nothing except sudden force.

Still watching Jenny's house, Junior lights a cigarette, sucking smoke past the hollow spot growing just behind his Adam's apple. He doesn't think about that quiet boy who'd sit in a chair all day with his mother, nursing her hangovers and wounds. Nor of his mother, who tried with all her heart to give as good as she got, but was never quite able to. Junior rolls the window down, hacks up a chunk of nicotine-fused phlegm, and spits it out the window.

And then he freezes.

The front door of Jenny's house cracks open and a man steps out. A young man with a goatee, wearing what looks like a mechanic's shop pants.

Junior starts his car, and the man jumps a little, and then starts walking quicker down the sidewalk to a beat-up Honda Accord that Junior hadn't even seen sitting there.

Then Junior's cell phone rings.

joy

Once Patterson has the bodies out of the trunk he can't stop grinning. He hits the highway and lets the Corvette open up, still shot through with Vicodin and adrenaline. He doesn't even try not to speed. He's pretty sure he can outrun any cop stupid enough to try to pull him over in the thing, anyway. The thought that he'll probably end up facing a murder charge if he is pulled over does occur to him, but there's no stopping it. Turns out there's no better medicine for heartache than surviving a murder attempt and stealing a car.

He makes Fort Garland before pulling out his cell phone and dialing Junior. "What the fuck do you want?" Junior answers in a rough whisper.

"I'm on my way to see you."

"I'm busy."

"Get unbusy."

"Does it really fucking need to be right now?"

"Yeah. It kind of does."

There's a long pause. "All right." Junior's voice sounds like chipped Sheetrock. "You coming by my house?"

Patterson hasn't thought that far ahead. "I don't think so. Anywhere else you can think of?"

"How far are you out?"

"At least three hours. Maybe four."

"You know where the Bar Bar is?" Junior asks.

"Downtown's probably not a good idea, either."

"Whatever your problem is, it's better in plain sight. You can trust me on that."

"If you say so." Patterson hangs up.

The Bar Bar is the one bar in Denver that opens at six o'clock in the morning, which is just about the time Patterson pulls up. It's a stucco box, right on the edge of downtown where the abandoned warehouses and gearhead mechanics take over. It's never had any name that anyone knows of, but there's a neon sign out front that says Bar, which is where people get Bar Bar from. From noon to close it's populated by homeless cart pushers and bitter Indians, but at six o'clock in the morning you're liable to see anybody. A high-end stripper killing the smell of baby oil and perfume with gin, a television lawyer blowing his last line of cocaine in the men's room, an overtime cop pounding bourbon before heading home to his impending divorce. Anybody.

Patterson takes a stool next to Junior, who is sitting by a homeless man with a beardful of coagulated blood. Junior looks at Patterson and shakes his head. "You're gonna need to tone it down some," he says. "I don't think I can take you glowing."

"It's love of life," Patterson says. "It's joy." He knocks back the shot of bourbon Junior has waiting for him. "Sorry to get you up in the middle of the night."

"I wasn't sleeping anyway." Junior slaps his pockets for his cigarettes. He finds them and pulls out the pack.

"You can't smoke in here," Patterson says. "Can't smoke in any of the bars in Denver. You're the one who told me that."

"True," Junior says, lighting his cigarette. "I don't give a shit."

"Hey," the bartender says. "Hey."

Junior ignores him.

"I'm talking to you, motherfucker," the bartender says. He's in his early thirties, with a mustache and a Hawaiian shirt. He doesn't look particularly tough, but he carries himself like someone who's taken more than his fair share of shit in his chosen occupation, and knows how to handle it. "No smoking at the bar, motherfucker. If you want to smoke, move outside."

"Call me motherfucker again and I'll put it out in your ear," Junior says.

"It's a term of endearment," the bartender says. "Put it out or go outside. I'm the one who gets the ticket, not you."

Junior lets the cigarette fall out of his fingers and scuffs it out on the floor with the toe of his cowboy boot. Patterson almost falls off his stool seeing him comply. Then he looks at Junior hard for the first time since walking into the bar. Junior looks like Patterson imagines he did just about thirty seconds after he survived Mel and the biker. Shell-shocked.

"All right," the bartender says. "You can get the hell out of here. I don't need your shit."

Patterson finds a twenty-dollar bill in his wallet. "How's that?" He offers it to the bartender.

The bartender studies the bill and slides it in his pocket. "No more of that shit," he says, pointing at Junior.

"No more of that shit," Patterson agrees.

"All right." The bartender walks away down the bar.

Patterson shakes his head and starts to say something to Junior. Then he starts to say something else. Then he decides on "Something wrong with you?"

"There ain't a fucking thing wrong with me, partner. You're the one who called me."

So Patterson tells him. Tells him all about it, from the minute Chase's woman and the biker show up at the cabin right to the hole he buried them in.

Junior looks near impressed. "You're a fucking killer."

"This is my last," Patterson promises.

"I recommend it," Junior says. "There's only so many places to bury a body in the great state of Colorado."

Patterson doesn't answer.

"But this ain't a problem, partner," Junior says.

Patterson looks at him. "It ain't?"

"Hell no," he says, pulling his cell phone out of his pocket. "This is an opportunity." He stands and takes his cell phone out the door to make a call.

idiot

They pull into Vicente's compound sometime in the midmorning. He waves them through the gate and around his junk barricades, to a parking spot by the garage. Junior and Patterson climb out of the car.

"How does it drive?" Vicente asks. "Does it drive well?"

"It does," Patterson says. "It ain't like nothing I've ever driven."

Vicente's fingers twitch open and closed. Behind his glasses his brown face is breaking all over in a grin and there's a kind of excited ruffling of the air emanating from him. Patterson sees a smirk flash on Junior's face, but it's gone when Vicente cuts a look back at him.

"She's beautiful," Vicente says. He circles the car, touching it here and there. Then he just stops and stares at the supercharger. "Seven minutes twenty-six point four seconds at Nürburgring," he says, in a hushed voice. "Did you know that? They call it the Green Hell. It's the most dangerous track in the world. And that's the fastest time ever posted by a production automobile. Ever." He turns to them, his eyes tearing up.

"Whatever the fuck you say," Junior says. "This is Patterson, by the way. You've got him to thank for it."

Vicente looks at Patterson for just a second, then says, "Thank you, Patterson. Come inside. Have a beer. I will pay you inside."

The air in the garage is thick with oil, floating with motes of dust. Vicente counts out two stacks of bills, ten thousand dollars apiece, and hands each of them a bottle of imported beer out of a shop refrigerator. They drink the beer while Vicente drives the Corvette into the garage and opens the hood. He's so excited it makes Patterson a little nervous.

After a little while, Patterson watches another man come into the garage. He is larger than Vicente, much larger, with a long, black ponytail and a face like an oncoming train. He says something to Vicente that Patterson can't hear, and then leans against the wall and watches the other Mexican for a few minutes.

"He's sociable, ain't he?" Patterson says to Junior.

"Don't worry about him," Junior says. "He ain't nothing but a big teddy bear."

"I don't think you mean that."

Junior stands. "I don't." He walks over to the man and they stand together, talking. The man's expression doesn't change, not even a little. Patterson expects him to separate Junior's head from his shoulders at any second. When he is done saying whatever needed to be said, Junior walks back over. "You can sleep on my floor," he says.

"Up to you. I feel fine. We can head back to the mesa now."

"I need sleep," Junior says. "And food. I know a place. I'll buy you a beer."

Even as good as he's feeling, Patterson opens his mouth to pro-test the idea of going into any establishment that serves alcohol with Junior. But before he can say anything, his phone rings. He looks at one of the walls for a second. Then he digs it out of his pocket. He holds it in his hand and lets it ring until it stops ringing.

But then it starts ringing again.

"Hello," he answers.

"Are you with Henry's son?" Laney says brightly.

"Just heading back now."

"You're an idiot," she says.

"It was kind of an emergency."

"One of the dumbest human beings I've ever met in my life," she continues.

"I'll be back this afternoon. Promise."

"Will you do me this favor?" she asks. "Will you call me when you get to the cabin? Just so I know you're alive. I don't think it's too much to ask, considering I'm the one who put you back together last time."

"I'll get some sleep and call you," Patterson says. "Maybe I'll buy a couple of chickens and pit-roast 'em."

"You think you can dig your way out of this one?"

"Your boy, Gabe. Does he know how to play catch?"

"You're really working," she says.

"I'll pick up a glove and a baseball," he says.

"Call me when you get there."

He hangs up.

"Henry?" Junior asks.

Patterson shakes his head, putting the phone back in his pocket.

"I didn't know you had other friends," Junior says.

"She ain't friendly," Patterson says.

"I got one of those, too."

visionary

Patterson and Junior don't leave right away, though. They sit in their chairs at the chess table and drink the shop beer. Watching Eduardo and Vicente as they move around the car. Vicente has a notebook in hand, and he's pointing things out to the other man. His excitement has calmed, and Patterson sees him now as he must be. Deliberate with whatever plans he's making for the car, but, at the same time, obviously tasking his partner with the details. He's the visionary of the two, Patterson realizes. And Eduardo, the one who looks like he'd win a fair fight with a dump truck, it's his job to make sure those visions are realized.

Then Patterson looks at Junior, who is looking at nothing. He tries to imagine how Junior fits between the two of them. Or if he does. And then he wonders why exactly it is that he called Junior instead of just dumping the car in a ditch somewhere. He has a practical answer. An atomic-orange Corvette ZR1 would draw attention anywhere on earth, but in the San Luis Valley it would draw only a little less than a UFO landing. But there's another answer, too, and he stops himself from thinking about it.

The adrenaline has dumped from him, and the good feeling he got from having survived Mcl and the biker, it's washing out quick. He tries to stop its full descent. He reminds himself how lucky he is again. How he really has no right to be sitting in this garage with a beer at all. But it doesn't do any good. And the shoveled-out feeling left in its place is another thing he can't think about.

"You've come around all the sudden," Junior says.

Patterson realizes what must have been on his face. "It's been a rough month," he says.

"It has," Junior agrees.

"It's gonna get rougher."

Junior nods. "It will."

Eduardo is holding the notebook now, and Vicente is instructing him on what to write. They're crouched down by one of the rear tires. "How the hell do they do it?" Patterson asks.

But Junior doesn't answer.

Justin

I haven't slept in more than a day, and I still can't. Even here on the couch. I can't stop thinking of you. And of a friend of mine, Chase. And his woman, Mel. It's the thought that she can't have possibly had any other reason for coming after Chase but that she missed him. Whatever he may have done to her, whatever he turned himself into, she missed him. It was a hole inside her that she couldn't fill. Whatever operation she was running, whatever she had going on, she burnt it all down to find a man who hogtied her in a bathtub. But now they're both gone, her and Chase. And there is no hole, nothing to miss. What they were to each other has disappeared as completely as if it never had been.

Junior's Border Patrol dealer, Carmichael, was wrong about one thing. Americans do disappear. All the time. They fall off the earth. That's something I've learned from working natural disasters. One sudden earthquake or flood and it's all gone. All the contracts that prove you own the things you think you own, your whole lifetime of accumulated paperwork to prove who you are. There were people who disappeared into FEMA prisons after Hurricane Katrina who weren't heard from for weeks or months. There were others who disappeared into the water like they never existed at all.

When you work disasters, you work with bodies. Not every time, not all the time, but you find yourself on disposal duty now and then. And, they don't tell you this when you sign up, but if you work clearing power lines long enough, you'll see more accidents than you can count, and some of them will be fatal. When you play with chain saws at great heights, it ain't hard to end up dead.

Sometimes I think Henry and Brother Joe have it exactly backward. The question isn't how to live off the grid, it's how to remain tied to it. Most of what you think is your life can be ruptured in an instant. If you don't believe me, ask any prison inmate. Maybe the real question isn't how to make the world forget you, maybe it's how to make it recognize you. Even your parenthood, your right to your own children, can be stripped from you at the whim of a bureaucrat.

And some just die.

I wasn't a very good father to you. I know that. I thought I had all the time in the world to become better than I was. I ripped through my time with you like I had it to burn. I drank most nights and told you to shut up when there was something on television I wanted to watch. I was worn down and hungover most days. Most of the time I was wishing I was doing anything other than playing with you.

But there was also story time. I did all right with story time, at least some nights. You huddled up under the covers and me stretched out on top of them. Usually with a beer in hand and my boots still on, which pissed your mother off to no end, but still I was there. In winters it'd get so cold that we could watch our breath while we talked, even with our old furnace clunking away. I'm a good storyteller. Or, at least, I like to tell stories. Most of them came from everyday shit I'd twist around for you until it was interesting.

I still feel like I'm telling you stories, like it's the only thing between you being here and not being here. That's something I have to hold on to, you being here. If I don't tell you these stories, I got nothing. If I stop, you're gone.

I was a good listener, too. At least I think I was. You had your Superman kick, where we had talks about whether or not he could fly without his cape. Then there was God. I don't know where that came from, but I told you everything I knew about the subject, which wasn't much. And then you told me everything you knew about the subject, which was considerably more, if not entirely canonical.

I can't even talk about God anymore.

Some nights we'd drift off to sleep in midconversation right there on the bed. You curled up under the covers and me laid out on top. Laney'd have to come in and wake me up, looking for somebody to talk to herself.

I hope it matters for something, some of that. There's times it's hard not to feel like all of that time didn't go down a hole with you when you died.

wickedest

It's almost impossible to measure the damage that damaged young men can do to themselves. Spending their nights drinking, doing whatever drugs they can afford, fumbling through the kind of endless and circular conversations only damaged young men can tolerate. Conversations so full of self-pity and self-hatred they can only end by the sudden imposition of physical force. A beer bottle through a window, a kitchen table smashed to pieces on the floor, an unanticipated fistfight. They feed on themselves, they feed on each other.

Then there's the next morning. The self-disgust from understanding that whatever it is that's burning you up, whatever's tearing you apart, it's no more unique to you than the color of your hair. Rough childhoods ain't mysteries, they're the building blocks of life. The day-to-day hell as lived by most everybody. The only thing that feels more pathetic than that you let it happen to you is that you allow it to break you in half now that you're free of it.

Junior doesn't know that he's really grown out of any of it. He's just grown so disgusted by the company of other people that he can't much abide being around anyone he could lie or complain to anymore. He's one of those few people who'd rather drink in the company of his own memories. Unfortunately, it's starting to seem like it's the only thing he can do.

He's not so far gone that he thinks he has any right to be angry with Jenny for getting herself a boyfriend. Fidelity has never been one of Junior's strong points. Even when Casey was a baby and they were as happy as they were ever going to be, there were still the runs down to El Paso, the whores Carmichael scared up. It's pretty hard to get mad at a woman for taking up with another man when you've given her no reason to stick with you. And Junior knows all of that. But it doesn't stop him from cruising by Jenny's house the next night, looking for that Honda Accord. Or the next night, either.

It's the second night, around eleven o'clock, that he spots it. And just like the last time, around two o'clock, here he comes out of her house, the little goateed motherfucker, wearing the same pants. Junior waits for him to get the lights on and get his car started, and he pulls out after him. Following from a distance, up the exit ramp onto I-70, and then down onto I-25, across town to Colfax Avenue.

Junior figures he knows him, then. Colfax Avenue was once described as the longest and wickedest street in America by *Playboy* magazine, and even as much as it's been tamed over the last decade, it still hosts enough prostitution and low-rent crime for any ten cities. Junior follows him down the run of cheap wino bars and flophouse motels, the kinds of places he used to stay before he began working for Vicente. The Motel Bar X. The Aristocrat. The Driftwood.

But the Accord doesn't stop. It keeps going, and before you know it they're in Lakewood. And now it's Home Depot and King Soopers. And Junior realizes he's never been this far down Colfax.

The Accord turns, driving back into a residential neighborhood, rows of the kind of cheap tract housing that has taken over every undeveloped acre around Denver. It stops in front of a shit-brown duplex, one with three or four other cars parked out front of it, and Junior realizes that the little son of a bitch lives with his parents. Junior parks a house or two down and almost laughs out loud. He almost calls Jenny on his cell phone just so he can laugh at her.

The man gets out and looks back at Junior's car. Junior can tell he doesn't know what to do. Whether to walk up on Junior or not. Junior lights a cigarette and lets him figure it out. And the man, for his part, finds a pack of cigarettes in one of the deep front pockets of his pants, and lights one of his own. Then he walks over to the stoop and sits down, smoking it, staring at Junior's car, at the point of light that is Junior's cigarette.

Then when he's done, he stubs it out and goes inside.

Junior doesn't leave right away. He sits there for a long time. He's not exactly sure what he's thinking, but he knows it's not good. Some of it's got to do with people he knows who'd set this house on fire for no more than he made selling the Corvette to Vicente. And some of it's got to do with his just skipping the middleman and burning it down himself.

But he doesn't. And when he's stopped shaking, he drives home.

disaster

Patterson finally does call Laney. He finishes out the week working for Paulson first, though. But come Saturday, he buys chickens, and even a baseball and a glove. And he digs a pit out back of the cabin and lines it with flat rocks and builds a fire in it. He's sitting on a rock by the fire with a can of Milwaukee's Best, scratching behind Sancho's ears, when he looks up and sees Henry standing next to him.

"What're you thinking about," Henry asks.

"I'm not thinking," Patterson says. "I'm kind of making a point of it."

Henry stands, leaning on his cane. "You going to tell me about it this time?"

"Probably not."

"Happens just about every time this year, doesn't it?" Henry says. "Not my son, but this exact pattern."

Patterson moves from scratching behind Sancho's ears to between his eyes. The old dog lets out a rumble of pleasure. "Just about."

Henry looks up at the sky. It's thin blue and there's no moisture at all. You can smell the dust, the heat, you can almost hear the reservoir sludging around low and thick at the bottom of the other side of the mesa. "You ever wonder about whether we've got any business being here at all?" he asks.

"All the time."

"White people, I mean."

"I know what you mean."

"There's whole towns just disappearing. Just gone. Maybe a couple of old-timers who ain't got nowhere to go are staying, but that's it. Even Denver's looking more and more like an island. On the other side, Indians are buying the land up and running new herds of bison."

Patterson's no longer scratching Sancho. Just rubbing his side. Sancho's eyes have closed and he's falling away into sleep.

"Turns out we never did know shit about living here," Henry continues.

"I've thought about it."

"It hasn't rained for shit in weeks," he continues. "And there was next to no snowfall last winter. That's a fact. People can't live without water, and sooner or later this place is going bone dry. You can't just make water out of nothing. We're going the way of the dinosaur."

"Good riddance," Patterson says. A dry wind blows around them. Patterson closes his eyes against the dust and leaves them closed for a little while, letting his hand settle on his dog's ribs, feeling him breathe. He's floating.

"You know Emma spends the night with me sometimes? She comes over and we eat dinner, and then she goes to bed with me. I pay her for that."

"It's none of my business."

"I can't even fuck," Henry continues. "Can't even get it up most of the time, and it hurts too much when I can. I pay her just to sleep with me. We don't call it that, paying for her to sleep with me, but I give her a hundred dollars every week and say it's for housework, above and beyond her real job."

"Well. Why the hell not?"

"You're missing the point. I'm not telling you about it to make you embarrassed, I'm telling you about it because you need to simplify your life. You're overcrowded and disappearing at the same time. You're a fucking disaster." He puts his hand on Patterson's shoulder, and he leaves it there for a while. Then he pulls it away. "You do good by them tonight," he says. "You're going to need their goodwill."

"I know it," Patterson says.

pause

After it gets dark, long after they've eaten the chickens and Patterson has passed the baseball with Gabe for a little while, he pours a gallon of gas over a pile of twisted piñon pine and sagebrush and lights it with a twig. There's a low boom, the wood flaring a sudden blue and yellow, and when Patterson looks over Gabe is giggling at him like no kid he's ever seen. Laney just shakes her head, but she's doing it in that way that means Patterson is just fine. That means something to Patterson. He knows what's coming.

Then Gabe falls asleep and they put him to bed up in the loft. And Laney's brought a joint, and Patterson is lying on his back in the dirt by the fire, his Avrilla sweatshirt for a pillow, and Sancho stretched out next to him. Laney sits cross-legged, scratching in the sandy dirt with a stick, her face veiled by her hair. He can feel her looking at him, and he knows what she's about to say before she says it.

"It's coming up," she says.

Patterson nods.

"I'm not going to bug you about it," she says. "But you could come with us if you wanted."

"I'll think about it."

"We usually put flowers on his grave and then eat pizza at Ha Ha's," she says. Then, after a pause that seems longer than it probably is, "We were hoping you could come."

"We?"

"Me," she says. "But Gabe would like you to come, too. He loves you. And he is Justin's brother."

"I'll think about it."

"You mean you'll think about it, but I'd better shut up."

"I mean I'll think about it."

"Okay," she says. She doesn't talk for a minute. "Why do you think Henry lives out here?"

"He thinks he'll be safe when the shit hits the fan. He's of the opinion the government's out to kill everybody, and they won't be able to get him here."

"Like the stuff on that radio show? Brother Joe?"

"Exactly like that."

"You know I listen to that show sometimes when you're on the road. I listen to it when I'm lonely for you."

Patterson looks at her.

Her forearms and hands are tan and dusty. She draws something in the dirt and then crosses it out. She cranes her neck toward her failed artwork. Her neck is as long and white as the belly of a snake, so faintly lined with veins that they seem to live just above her skin.

Something cold runs down Patterson's sun-battered face, and he knows he's in trouble. He starts to say something, probably something stupid, just to stick a knife in the moment and let the air out of it, but she beats him to it. "Do you want to know what I think? About why people believe all those things?"

"Tell me," he says.

"I think it's about loss. That when you lose someone or something important there's a hole that gets left where it used to live inside of you. I think that's where all of those conspiracy theories come from. It's like there's a bottomless hole in the people that believe them and they can't tell anybody about it, because it's only a hole, so they make up stories just as awful and terrifying as it is. They throw all these things down into it, hoping to fill it up."

Patterson refuses to take the bait. He turns his head away and watches the sparks from the fire flutter briefly in the updraft before being extinguished by the inky sky, bobbing along to their end. Like he knows that it's time to make his exit, Sancho whines, rises, and wanders off out of the firelight. Patterson watches him go.

"And do you know why you live up here?" she continues.

"Because it's cheap," Patterson says. "Because most of the time people leave me alone."

She shakes her head. "It's because you won't let anything fill the hole that's in you. And that's not any better."

Then she's on top of him, her breath hot with marijuana and tobacco. She's running her hands over his face, kissing him in bursts. And he's jamming his hands up her shirt, clamping her against him, pawing under her jeans. Her hands following, unzipping his jeans. She's dehydrated and dry from the weed, but they fuck in the dirt, making it through with water and spit. And when they're done they collapse in a heap. But there's none of the urgency gone, and nothing is changed.

• • •

After Laney is up in his loft, asleep with Gabe, Patterson sits outside on the porch. The Blanca Massif is obscure against the night sky, a black and broken patch of sky, somehow hidden, as if eclipsing the moon. Patterson thinks of Snippy again, the horse that became the first mutilation. He's seen spooked horses before. Seen them here on the mesa, seen them with Henry. The duck and the sideways bolt, the head flinging back. And Patterson thinks of Snippy in a way that he never has before. Of what it must have been like to be that mare. Whatever she was taken by, it was alien to her, and Patterson doubts whether there could even have been a measure to her terror. To her, there wouldn't be the slightest difference between a helicopter and a spaceship.

There's times he wishes the porch had been built to face some other direction. Maybe south, out of the valley. But it wasn't, so he sits there and stares north and breaks all over inside.

Justin

Most of the time I can't stop seeing your face. And most of the time I make sure of it. I write to you because it forces me to pull you up out of my memory and hold you in front of me. It's that nightmare about looking for something that I can't find and then realizing it's you. I know that if I don't keep writing you'll sink down so far I won't be able to pull you up anymore. You'll go under for good and I'll be left holding what everybody else has. A memory of a very nice little boy who is gone. But you're not gone for me.

The only time I can't lift you out is now. Right now. As we get nearer to the anniversary of your death I can't find your face anywhere. It happens every year. It doesn't matter how hard I grope around, you're just not there.

But he is. Court is. Where I'm looking for you, I can't help but find him.

The first anniversary, I thought I had to kill him to get you back. As we got nearer to the date and I couldn't find anything but him in my mind, that's what I arrived at. That the only way to clear him out of my head, to get you back, was to wipe him off the planet. And not with a gun, either. Nothing as neat as a bullet. I planned to beat him to death with my fists.

It was your mother who stopped me. It was a phone call with her. I told her the whole thing. How I couldn't drive Court out of my head. How I could pick up a picture of you, stare at it, and then put it down and forget what you looked like in twenty seconds. How I couldn't sleep anymore for being scared I'd forget you altogether.

She explained that it was happening to her, too. That it was the anniversary, that it was trying to bury our memories of your life with your death. She told me that she was sure it would pass. That the anniversary was like a moon drawing our memories in a tide, but that it would pass. She convinced me that it would be no different for Court. That there was nothing I could do to punish him worse than that itself. She convinced me to leave him alone.

shitass

The thing about going for three or four days without sleep at a stretch, running on cocaine and fumes, is that when sleep does finally hit, it hits like a sledgehammer. Which is how Junior ends up passed out behind the wheel of his car, parked on the street with a good view of Jenny's house.

That is, until somebody slaps the window his head is rested against. Then he tries to jump in three directions at once, banging his head on the doorframe, then swatting away the cigarette that's burnt down between his fingers.

When he looks out the window and sees Jenny's face, he thinks about just putting his keys in the ignition and driving away. But he doesn't. He rolls down the window and tries on his best grin. "How you doing, lady?"

"Unlock the door," she says.

He reaches across to the passenger's side and pulls the lock while she walks around the car. "What are you doing outside my house?" she asks, stepping into the Charger.

He rubs sleep out of his good eye, then lifts his eye patch and takes his handkerchief out of his pocket and rubs at his bad eye. "Sleeping."

"Don't get smart with me, Junior," she said. "Sure as hell not right now."

Junior finds a half-full beer between the seats and takes a drink. It's warm and flat.

"Don't stall, Junior," she says. "What're you doing spying on me?"

He shrugs.

"Junior?"

He takes another drink of the beer. Gags on it a little, but swallows.

"Junior?"

"You want the truth?"

"I want the truth," she says. "That's all I want."

"The truth is I got no idea."

She nods. "I guess that's about the only thing I'd believe."

Junior knows he should keep his mouth shut. But he can't quite yet. "Your boyfriend lives with his parents."

She looks at him.

"That's all I'm saying about it. If you're gonna get yourself a boy-friend, at least find one who can take care of my daughter."

"How do you think you're doing at that, Junior? Taking care of your daughter?"

It's Junior's turn to be silent.

"I'm not gonna apologize, Junior."

"I ain't asking you to."

"I mean it. Not for anything. Not for moving, not for getting a job, and not for anybody I see. You ain't got no right to say anything about my life."

"I know." He takes another drink of the warm beer and wipes his mouth with the back of his hand. "But you can do better than some shitass who wears his uniform pants on a date."

"Jesus, Junior." She just stares at him, her shadow-battered face bending in on itself in the street light. He tries not to look at her, but can't help it. "What the hell are you gonna do with yourself?"

He shrugs.

"What you're doing ain't working. Just so you know. I know you think it is, but it ain't."

Junior picks up the beer again as if to take another drink, but decides against it and drops the can out the window.

Her voice softens. "You're welcome to be around as much as you want, Junior. I meant what I said. Once I start working I can help you find something else besides the driving. And you can see Casey, anytime."

"How's about if I want to just sit out here and watch the house," he says.

"That, too," she says. She reaches over and puts her hand on his cheek, and he bends his head into it. "We miss you, Junior. I don't think you know it, but we do." Then she opens her door and steps out, walks back toward her house.

Junior watches her go. Watches her all the way up to her door, to where she disappears inside the house.

And for just a second he thinks about following her.

almost

So Patterson hunkers by a neighboring gravestone and watches Laney and Gabe. Laney's wearing black. Black jeans and a black shirt and a short black leather jacket, which does nothing but make Patterson realize that he isn't wearing anything black at all. Justin's stone is just on the edge of a small cottonwood grove, and even as thin and under-watered as the trees are, they tower over the small, plain gray marker.

Patterson didn't have much to say about where they picked the cemetery. It was one in a hundred things that he didn't give a shit about when his boy died. But he was glad now that Laney picked it where she did. He doesn't think he's ever been in the place when it wasn't brown. The brown adobe walls around it, the brown iron gate, the brown halfhearted wood crosses that still weed the grounds, and the untended brown dirt in the place of grass. The Chinese elm shoots that have taken over half of Taos, even they're brown. There's something steadying about all the brown.

The fact is, Patterson's having the old panic attacks again. Sweating, heart surging, vision slipping. It's like no time has passed at all since Justin died, like it happened just today. He's using every single trick he knows to create distance between himself and it. And not just all the distractions he's created over the last month, all the distractions he's always created. He dry-swallows two more Vicodin and rests his arm on Sancho's back. Vicodin helps with that distance.

Laney's saying something and holding flowers in both her hands that she means to place on the grave. Which makes no sense to Patterson. What boy wants flowers? Gabe, he seems to know better, and he has two comic books rolled up in his fist that he means to leave. For the first time, Patterson is thankful for the boy. Thankful and sorry for him, too, as he watches his mother begin to cry.

Patterson wishes he could do what Laney needs him to. Not for the first time, he wishes he could be someone other than he is. He scratches Sancho between the shoulder blades. The dog, who he knows is standing there solid because he knows Patterson needs him there. Holding on to Sancho, Patterson's almost able to convince himself that he, at least, won't do the one thing that he knows will make this harder for Laney.

Almost.

contracting

Nights in Junior's house are spent wandering the halls, pacing the living room and bedroom. Whatever cocaine he's done coursing through his system, jolting him awake at the slightest noise. Even changes in the air currents in the house can wake him up, and he'll try every spot he can to get some rest. Tonight it's been the bed, then the couch, then the floor of the bedroom between the bed and the wall, where the hardwood floor is cool on his back. That's where he is, on the floor of his bedroom, when he wakes with the feeling something has changed in the air outside the open bedroom door.

Then he hears the front door close very quietly, and he's all the way awake.

One other thing about sleeping on the floor in his bedroom, it's under his bed that Junior keeps his Mossberg autoloader. In his line of work, it isn't as though he hasn't considered the possibility of home invaders. He turns just on his side, so he can see the door of the bedroom, and eases the shotgun to his shoulder, sliding it so the ghost ring sights cover the bottom six inches of the opening into the living room. A pair of tennis shoes and about four inches of khaki pants appear.

The Mossberg holds seven rounds of 00 buckshot, each of them containing nine pellets of .33 caliber ball. Unlike a pump shotgun, the autoloader can unload those rounds as fast as Junior can pull the trigger.

And he does, pulling the trigger as fast as he can. The shotgun's report is so loud it blows holes in his hearing, yellow punctures of sound and light. But Junior barely hears any of it once he begins shooting. Time slows and his vision narrows and the pellets drive smoke and tissue and blood and sock and khaki from the man's ankles, from the bones. There's something like a shriek, though Junior can't hear well enough to be sure. Then the man's falling, and Junior shoots him in the face. It makes a scooped bowl of loose gore of the top half of the man's head, and Junior doesn't bother firing again. There's nothing of the man but a sack of blood emptying on the floor.

Junior grabs his Glock from the end table and waits. When his hearing finally clears, or at least calms to a dull ring, and he detects nothing else from the house, he steps out from behind the bed. The mess is incredible, blood and bits of the man coat the floor and the walls behind him. And the smell's worse. Coppery blood and feces. Junior notes the tattoos, the black hair, the patches of brown skin on the man.

He walks to him, his bare feet slopping in the blood, and pulls his pockets. No wallets, no ID. Nothing but a little black leather book. Junior opens it, and even with his bad Spanish, he's able to translate the passage: It is better to be a master of one peso than a slave of two; it is better to die fighting than on your knees and humiliated; it is better to be a living dog than a dead lion.

Junior hangs his head, squatting there in the blood. He sees the rest of his life like through a tunnel. And it's contracting fast, shrinking so that he can see right through to the end. He has to put a hand down in the blood to steady himself.

There's no way he's getting away from this. Even in Junior's neighborhood, emptying a shotgun in your bedroom will bring a phone call to the police. Meaning he's got somewhere around twenty minutes to figure out what he wants to do with the rest of his fast-compressing life.

His first thought is to make a run for it. Maybe north, to get lost in Montana. Maybe south to Mexico.

His second thought is to make sure that those who've played fast and loose with the rest of his life, that they understand what that means.

gentle

"**I** know it's hard, honey," Laney says to Patterson. Gabe is in bed. He's fallen asleep on the car ride home, worn out from Laney feeding him stories about his brother.

"I'll leave in a minute," Patterson says. He's tilting against Laney's sink, drinking a water glass of bourbon from a bottle that he probably left there. The sink has dirty dishes and dead flies in it.

"I don't want you to leave," she says. She sits hunched forward on a cushioned chair at the small writing desk where she does bills. "I want you to stay. That's what I want you to do."

The whiskey is a small fire in his solar plexus. "I don't know how you do it," Patterson says.

"People survive, honey," she says. "Why don't you go in and look in on Gabe? Look in on him sleeping."

Patterson finishes the bourbon. He knows it's time to leave.

"Look in on him while he's sleeping," she says. "It'll help."

Patterson pushes off the sink. "I've got to go."

"Don't go." She stands, steps toward him. Patterson puts the palm of his hand in the middle of her chest and pushes her back. He isn't as gentle as he could be. "Patterson," she says. She steps toward him again. He shoves her back again. "Don't be stupid," she says. "Stay."

He moves toward the door, but she's there. He puts out his hand to move her aside. She slips it. "I've got to go," he says. He hears panic in his voice. He shuffles to the side, steps forward. She's there again in front of him. He shoves her out of the way. She bangs into the cupboard by the door. The dishes inside click together. "I've got to go," he says again.

Her face blotches red. "You're not going." She slaps him on the forehead. She probably means to hit him on the mouth, but she's out of practice. She tries again and gets him on the chin. He stiff-arms her into the writing desk. A cup of pens turn over, clattering out onto the floor. She pushes off the desk, swinging with her open hands. Right on his cheek, left on his jawline, right across his eye. Then she closes her fists and flurries him. She tires finally. She drops her hands and stands with her shoulders hunched, breathing hard like an animal.

Patterson smacks her openhanded on the side of the head. She cries out, curls her face into her shoulder. She swings tentatively back at him. He grabs her hand out of the air and hits her on the other side of the head. She flails with her free hand. Patterson catches it, shoves her backward into the desk again. The chair hits the floor, the cushion falling free of the seat. "I'm going," he says.

"You better not go." She's breathing heavy. "You motherfucker."

weakness

It's early morning, but they're in the garage with the door open, the heavy fan set into the wall pounding tirelessly at the acrid air. Eduardo's under the hood of the Corvette and Vicente's sitting at the chess table with one leg crossed over the other. He's wearing a long underwear shirt covered in oil stains, drinking an espresso and reading the *New York Times*. He looks up at Junior and nods, but doesn't say anything. He sips his espresso and returns his attention to the newspaper. The sun through the windows lies in dusty yellow blankets on the floor. Then Eduardo turns. "Hello Junior," he says.

"A man came in my house," Junior says.

Eduardo leans over and picks up a rag and wipes his hands. "A man?"

"A man."

Vicente folds his paper and sets it down on the table. He places his espresso cup on top of it. "Did he mean you harm?" He asks it in a serious voice.

Junior nods. He starts to say something, but his voice thickens in his throat. Then he says, "I blew him inside out."

Eduardo doesn't say anything.

"I unloaded a shotgun into him," Junior says. "By the time I was done you could've fit him in a dustpan."

Eduardo finishes wiping his hands. He tosses the rag in the dirt. "Junior took his friend with him down to El Paso," he says to Vicente. "Just took him along for the ride. This is what Carmichael told me."

Junior pulls the little black leather book out of his front pocket and shows it to them. "This is one of their books," he says.

"He is never sober," Eduard continues. "He will have us both in jail or dead."

"What did you do, Eduardo?" Vicente says softly.

"He is weak," Eduardo says. "Not only weak. Weak and stupid. You think because he is charming, he is smart. But he is not."

"Did you try to have this boy killed?" Vicente says.

"I am not the one to worry about," Eduardo says.

"It was La Familia?" Vicente asks. "You contacted them."

"This was a risk of working with La Familia," Eduardo says. "I warned you of this, Vicente. I warned you of it and you let him into your house. He preyed on your weakness. Your considerable weakness."

Vicente just shakes his head.

Eduardo holds his hands out. "Have you thought about what would have happened to us?" he says to Junior. "To Vicente?"

"I thought about it all the way over," Junior says.

Eduardo opens his mouth to say something else, but Junior has his Glock out of his holster and does his best to put the bullet right down Eduardo's throat. The hollow point round misses, but just slightly, catching him through the right eye. It expands, fragmenting in the tissue and skull, and everything to the side of Eduardo's eye blows off his skull in a vapor. He staggers toward Junior. Juniors drops the front sight and fires three rounds into his chest. Eduardo crumbles forward in a heap. Blood spits from his head, from his mouth, from his nose.

Junior's never heard anything like the sound that comes out of Vicente. It's something like the scream of a monkey. He hurtles from his chair, his hands clawing at Junior's eyes. Junior punches into his chest with the Glock, fires two rounds right into his sternum. Vicente's nails rake Junior's cheeks, taking chunks of skin and flesh.

Junior tries to move backward, to give himself some room. Vicente keeps coming. Junior stumbles over a toolbox. He falls, firing upward into Vicente's body. Vicente jumps at Junior. His glasses are broken, blood frothing from the corners of his mouth and his nose. Junior slams the Glock into his side, under his arm, and fires twice more.

It's the second round that stops Vicente. Junior doesn't know what he hits, but Vicente's face freezes and he stops moving, blood spilling out of the hole in his side. Then the muscles in his face slacken and he's dead.

Junior grunts and shoves Vicente off him. He stands, looking around.

sorry

Dr. Court still lives in the same little adobe house, near downtown Taos. He bought another place up in the ski country, but his main house is in Taos. When Patterson rings the doorbell, it takes a few minutes for him to answer. Long enough that Patterson starts to wonder if he finally left town.

But then he hears him fumble with the lock.

Patterson lets him get the door wide enough open that Court can see his face, then he shoves it all the way open with his knee and punches the old man square in the nose. Court falls back hard, landing with a muffled thump. Patterson lunges, looking to give him a boot in the side, but he's already rolling across the wood floor, his dark robe swirling in a tornado of fabric, slamming into the umbrella stand.

Patterson comes after him, too slow. Court's already on his feet, swinging a hickory cane. The knob explodes into the side of Patterson's jaw, sets every nerve ending in his head screaming. Patterson ducks the second swing and it punches through the drywall. Patterson catches the third swing on his forearm, grabs the cane with both hands, and yanks. Court lets go and the knob smashes into Patterson's nose. Something back in his nasal cavity snaps like a dry twig and blood sheets down his face.

Patterson jabs the cane at the old man, who sidesteps easily. He's moving fast, faster than any man of his age has any right to. Patterson throws the cane at his head and he snatches it out of the air. He readies it in his hands, but before he can fall back into a fighting stance, Patterson plows into him center-mass with his shoulder.

They fall together on the wood floor. Patterson lands on top of him. He plants his left elbow in Court's solar plexus and rears back to punch him, but both of Court's hands shoot out, take Patterson by the back of his neck, and he head-butts Patterson square in the mouth. Teeth break. Patterson spits bone and blood on Court's face and Patterson grabs him by the throat with his right hand.

Patterson squeezes down on him. It's like holding on to a boa constrictor, but he holds on. That stops him from dodging. Patterson chokes the old man, he chokes him hard, and when Court stops moving, Patterson punches him three times in the nose, feeling it break, and then climbs off him and sits with his back against the wall.

After five or ten minutes Court stirs and crawls his way to the wall opposite Patterson. Both of his eyes are filling with blood, his nose is crushed, and there are a series of gashes in his forehead from Patterson's teeth. Patterson spits tooth fragments out of his mouth. He tries not to swallow his tongue. "You motherfucker," Patterson slurs.

"I'm getting married," Court says. His voice is hoarse and swollen. He breathes heavily.

"You motherfucker."

"I'm so sorry." He's crying, the cocksucker. "This has to stop."

Patterson leers at him through the blood. "Or what?"

Court pulls a baby Glock from the underside of a hallway end-table, the duct tape he'd used to affix it in place looping away in a curl. "Or you'll have to kill me."

Patterson stumbles to his feet. "See if I don't."

"I can't do this anymore," Court says. He's still crying. "Nobody deserves this."

"You do," Patterson says.

robots

Later, much later, Junior sits on Casey's bed and watches her sleep. He's climbed in through the window. Her five-year-old face seems to have plumpened in her sleep, her eyes swelling behind the lids. She looks like some exotic fruit, ripe almost to bursting, just waiting to be bruised.

Then Junior feels bad for thinking of her as a fruit. Then for everything, right up until now. And for knowing that he won't see her again, and there's nothing he has that he can leave her to make her life any easier.

Junior loves her so much that it makes his bones go soft when he thinks about it. But there's nothing that'll make you hate yourself like having a child. Nothing to better expose all the holes in the person you've been telling yourself you are for your whole life. And when you make the mistakes a parent will make, even parents who aren't Junior, the guilt eats at the edges of those holes until there's nothing left but the holes.

He looks at her face. Plentiful and delicate. He sits on the bed and wells with guilt and love. And some other things, too.

Her eyes flicker open. "Daddy?"

"Hey, baby." He puts his hand on her cheek and then on her forehead. It's clumsy and blocklike, his hand. Not only the beer, but whiskey, too. And cocaine.

She yawns. "I was having a dream about robots," she says.

"Good robots or bad robots?"

"Robots are always good. It was the witches that were bad. But you were there to protect me."

"That's my job."

"That's what Mommy says her job is, too." Her nose wrinkles. "Your breath stinks."

"It happens when you grow up. Your breath stinks more."

"I know," she says. "Yours is worse than most grown-ups."

Junior laughs out loud. And then he stops. Those nights when Henry would come home, drunk and feeling sorry for himself. Junior'd hide so Henry couldn't hold on to him, crying and breathing whiskey all over him.

It occurs to Junior that there's nowhere to run. In the United States, it's prison. In Mexico, it's La Familia. It's almost a relief, knowing that there are no more questions. That his life is down to one choice. And all he can think of is Henry. Henry, who up until now has managed to take Junior's campaign of minor terror and fold it into his own story of himself.

"I don't care about your breath," Casey says. "Give me a kiss and I'm going back to sleep."

darker

Patterson's chewing Vicodin with broken teeth, swallowing blood and tooth fragments. He stops at the Questa Stop & Go for beer and drives out of New Mexico into Colorado, past the mesa, through San Luis, the valley rolling by in a long, aching blur. He drives with the window down. He drives fast, too fast, working his way through the first twelve-pack of beer, doing whatever he can to keep the night's fog over his mind. He drives pumping at the wheel, sometimes punching the dash. Then it dies down and he just drives. Left on 160 at Fort Garland, through Alamosa. Into the Rio Grande National Forest, up into the San Juan Mountains. It's dark in the San Luis Valley, it's darker in the San Juans. The flat black nothing of the valley floor trading in for the ragged black of the passing alpine forest. Deep into the night. Now and then a car, a pinpoint of light off in the distant black, a flash. The flare of his lighter illuminating the cab in a quick burst, gone. The coal burning red against the green dash lights.

Then there's a side road, then another. Dirt. Banging the truck over the ruts. Then, at the top of a rise, a place to stop. A valley below, more mountain above. He climbs out of the car, bringing his pack of cigarettes and the rest of the beer, and stretches out on the hood of the car and waits for the sun to rise.

Then he's awake. He's been asleep somehow and he's awake. The sun breaking over the mountains, ricocheting through the fog over the lodgepole pines and reflecting off the windshield, an explosion of light. His mouth as hard and dry as if he'd spent the night chewing cement mix. He turns to the side, scorching his cheek on the hood, and retches a string of stomach bile off the truck. Then finds his pack of cigarettes accordioned in his front pocket. He straightens one out and lights it, the smoke ripping over his broken teeth and hitting his lungs like a wood rasp.

He can't see the Blanca Massif from where he is. And he looks around and realizes that he can't see anything he knows. That's what drinking and driving is for. For blowing everything you're used to seeing into the rearview mirror, for bolting from all the shit that builds up in you, if only for your time on the road. And for Patterson, the thing that was building up against him is the Blanca Massif. He'd realized that just after leaving Court's house.

The problem being that when he tries to recollect how he got to where he is, there's nothing. Not a street sign, a turn. Nothing but that he's pretty sure he was heading west. And he realizes that his road atlas is in his Alice pack, back on the mesa.

Then his cell phone rings. He pulls it from his pocket, staring at it in disbelief that he has a signal. He accepts the call.

"Where are you?" Junior asks.

"The San Juans," Patterson says. "Somewhere."

"The San Juans. You want to know where I am?"

"The San Luis Valley?"

"The San Luis Valley. I been thinking about our conversation the other night."

"What conversation?"

"About Henry. About your confusion as to who the motherfucker is." A lighter flicks in the background. "I thought I'd come down and give you a lesson."

"No lesson needed. Besides, there's no telling when I'll be back on the mesa."

"If I were you, I'd drive fast." Junior disconnects.

blood

Patterson drives up the winding dirt road onto the mesa, into the low stars and the lower darkness. The constellations rise in crystalline explosions, endless and dizzying with alcoholic clarity. He drives like somebody falling in and out of sleep, yanking the wheel, and finally brings the truck to a stop behind Junior's Charger in Henry's barn's gravel lot. Where he opens the glove compartment and pulls out his .45.

The first thing as he comes around the barn is the smell. Blood and something else. Something heavy and wet and fertile, something he only remembers back in his snake brain, something that reminds him of Justin. Then there is the flickering of a nearly dead fire a few yards on the other side of the fence, barely illuminating a pile of gnarled brush. And a strange, wet, snuffling sound.

Patterson hops the fence into the pasture and almost lands on the body of a dog, a single leaking hole between its eyes. Patterson stops and looks down at the dog. Then, not quite believing what he sees, leans over so he's close enough that there can be no mistake.

It's Sancho. And all the sounds and smells of the night disappear. Patterson feels like he's stepped suddenly into a pressure chamber. He can't move and he can't speak for it all pressing in on him. But he knows he's out of options now, if he ever had any. So he stifles a round of dry heaves and forces his hands to stop shaking.

Then he makes his way toward the fire, into the flickering light and the shadow. Seeing as he closes the distance a man's form, squatting in the dirt and holding on to his knees. His head bowed, his face dripping blood into the dust. "Henry?" Patterson says.

Off beyond the fire, something rises out of a lake of shifting shadow. It's Junior, his Glock outstretched one-handed at Henry's head. "Throw some of that wood on the fire," he says in a thick voice.

Patterson doesn't move.

Junior flicks the muzzle of the gun at his father's head. "You better tell him," he says.

Henry turns his head to Patterson very slowly, and when he does, Patterson feels his muscles flush through and go weak. There's a silver dollar–sized puddle of gore where Henry's left eye had been. "Do what he says," Henry rasps.

"Did you drive fast?" Junior asks.

Patterson concentrates on his breathing, keeping the front sight of his .45 on Junior's chest. "You shouldn't have killed my dog, Junior."

"I didn't," Junior says. He reaches in his pocket and pulls out Chase's Kel-Tec .380, only about as big as the palm of his hand. "Henry did. Wasn't even hard to make him do it. You'd be surprised how quick he folds."

"It was me or him," Henry says. Blood drools out of his eye socket down his cheek. "He was going to shoot me if I didn't."

Junior raises his shoulders as if to say I told you so. "Set that gun down and put some wood on that fire," he says to Patterson.

"You'll only get one round off," Patterson says to him. "You ain't getting me."

"Please," Henry says. "I ain't ready for this."

"I'm not planning on getting you, Patterson," Junior says. "I kind of like you."

"Please," Henry says.

"Put it down, partner," Junior says. "This is going to play out either way. No need to rush it."

Junior's only about ten feet from Henry. Even if Patterson hits him perfectly, he'll be able to get his shot off at Henry, if he has the will to do so. And that's the one thing about Junior that Patterson doesn't doubt, his will to kill Henry. Patterson crouches, sets his gun in the dirt, then walks to the pile of wood and tosses a couple of crooked piñon sticks into the fire.

The dry wood catches immediately, popping and sparking in a short rush that allows Patterson to see what he hadn't been able to see before. The mare panting and exhausted in the dirt, the afterbirth soaking into the ground. The foal collapsed forward, its body slick and ethereal in the firelight and its coat spackled with dust.

"Where's Emma?" Patterson asks. "Did you kill her, too?"

He shakes his head. "Little bitch run off somewhere."

"You shouldn't have killed Sancho," Patterson says.

"I told you I didn't," he says. "Henry did. Besides, he bit my leg."

"Henry just pulled the trigger," Patterson says. "You killed my dog."

"You don't believe that," he says.

"Well. What's next?" The mare snorts, snorts again, and scrabbles upward in a sideways motion until she is standing. The umbilical cord between her and the foal breaks away and Junior shrugs.

"We keep going where it takes us," he says. He raises his gun and takes aim at the foal. But just as he's squeezing the trigger, a small rock swings out of the darkness, like on a string, and smashes into his temple. He reels sideways a step and swings the gun out at the night, flipping blood from his head in an arc. "You cunt," he calls. "I will fucking kill you when I get hold of you."

Another rock floats in from the side. A glancing blow on the back of the head. He slaps where it hit like he's been stung and turns back to the foal, which is now struggling to stand alongside the mare. The next rock comes from behind, crashing into the base of Junior's neck. It knocks him forward, almost on top of Henry. Henry makes a feeble grab at his leg. Junior kicks at the old man.

That's all Patterson needs. He dives onto Junior's back and all three of them collapse forward in the dirt.

Then there's a howl from out in the darkness, and Emma barrels into the light, her lips white and her mouth open wide. She swings a rock down double-fisted at Junior's head, but Junior jerks sideways and the rock hits Patterson on the shoulder instead. His arm goes instantly numb.

Junior kicks free and grabs the rock in Emma's hand, slamming it back into her face. She explodes blood. Patterson stumbles to his feet, holding his arm, staggering for the gun. But by the time he has his hand on it, Junior is standing with his boot on Emma's throat, his Glock pointed at her forehead.

"Shoot him," Henry slobbers. "Shoot him, Patterson."

"He's a brave one, ain't he?" Junior says. "He wasn't telling you to shoot me when it was his head, was he?"

"Shoot him," Henry says again.

Junior ignores Henry. "You're something, you little bitch," he says to Emma, leaning forward on the boot on her throat. She coughs, her face plumping like a balloon being squeezed from one end.

"Shoot him," Henry says again, and Patterson has to stop himself from shooting Henry instead.

"Go ahead," Junior says, reading Patterson's face.

The pasture is spinning out from under Patterson. Their voices so thick and weird he can barely understand them at all anymore. All he can hear is the throbbing in his shoulder, and what feels like broken glass moving under his skin when he moves it. This is shock, he thinks to himself, that's all this is. But thinking it does no good. He crumples to his knees.

"I told you he didn't change," Junior says. "Quitting drinking wasn't quitting anything for him. It was just more of Henry's horse-shit about Henry."

"This ain't me," Henry says. "You can't put everything on me, son."

"Shut up, Henry," Junior says mildly. "This ain't about you, dumb motherfucker." He squats down by Patterson. "How's the shoulder?" he asks in a low voice, almost conspiratorially.

Patterson can smell the whiskey on him, see the cocaine residue around his nose. His handsome face isn't handsome now, and Patterson doesn't think it's coming back. It's swollen and discolored, as though something has torn loose inside his head and flooded him. "It hurts," he says.

Junior's whole face seems to close and open again like a blind. He tilts a little in his squat, then rights himself. "You want me to check and see if it's broke?"

"There ain't no need to check."

"I guess not." Junior grins at him. "Seems like I'm always patching you back together."

"Is that how it seems to you?"

"If there was any other way, I would have done it," Junior says. "If there was any way at all."

Then a hole appears in Junior's throat. A small hole, almost like a large mosquito bite. He and Patterson look at each other, stupefied, registering the sound of the gunshot. Then Junior wobbles, grabbing at his throat, gurgling at the blood and saliva stringing out of his mouth. The second bullet punches through his jaw, leaving a small, jagged hole of tissue and bone. Finally understanding what's happening, he swings to his father, raising his pistol, but Henry empties the rest of the Kel-Tec's magazine into Junior's face.

Patterson hears someone grunt who sounds like himself. He jerks to move for Junior, but the pain in his shoulder rends his consciousness. Then he's back, and he's fumbling at the blood on Junior's face. He's wiping it away with the thumb and fingers of his good hand, and finds what's causing the blood. They're little more than leaking dimples, the bullet holes. And Patterson realizes that's not what he's looking for. That what he is looking for in Junior's face, it's no longer there.

"It fell out of his pocket when we were wrestling," Henry says. "Jesus, Patterson, he didn't give me no choice."

Patterson gropes for his .45 and raises it on Henry.

"Go ahead," Henry says. "If you think you got the right, you go ahead. You son of a bitch."

Patterson drops his gun in the dirt and holds on to his shoulder. Out of the corner of his eye, he sees Emma crawl across the dirt and collapse on Henry. Henry pulls her mangled face to his chest and holds it. "It's over, honey," he says. "We got him. We got the poor bastard."

Behind Henry and Emma, off the north edge of the mesa, the five peaks of the Blanca Massif look like earth torn out of the sky. Patterson wishes that he could just lie down right there, but he can't. Breathing tears ropes of pain down his broken shoulder, his lungs ripping free of his rib cage. Every breath pins him in place.

Then Henry is helping him up by his good arm. "Me, too," he's saying. "Me, too."

Justin

I haven't seen Henry since we buried Junior. I never went to visit him again, and he never came by the cabin. Now that the summer's over, I guess we both know where we stand. I know what Junior was. I probably know it as well as anyone. And Henry's right, everything wrong with Junior wasn't his fault. Junior didn't turn out the way he did because his daddy was a piece of shit. At least not only because of that. There was plenty wrong with Junior that Henry had nothing to do with.

But I ain't gonna give Henry any kind of justification for what he did. He doesn't deserve it any more than Court does. Or than I do for what I did to Chase and Mel. Reasons and justifications don't mean shit.

I went to see your mother one more time, though. Just yesterday, in fact. I drove into Taos for supplies and stopped by her house. She and the boy were sitting in the yard at the picnic table. Every light in the house was on behind them, and they were eating hamburgers on paper plates, talking over their food and laughing.

I sat in my truck for a long while watching them. I was far enough back that they couldn't see me, almost all the way around the bend in the road. There was a wind blowing. It was one of those fitful late summer winds, stopping and starting like it might come on strong at any minute, like it just might blow their little dinner party right out of existence. But you wouldn't have known it from them. Both in short-sleeved shirts, eating and laughing.

Then the wind kicked up a cloud of dust between me and them. It's been a long, dry summer, and there's not much left to keep the soil in place. And when the dust cleared, Laney was sitting motionless at the table, her hands in her lap, staring my way. The boy was still talking, still laughing, he hadn't seen me. But your mother was just staring. Then the boy caught what she was looking at and he stopped talking and just stared, too.

She said something to him and then walked out to me. I rolled down my window and waited for her.

"Hello, stranger," she said. "I was thinking about that yesterday. That it was getting close to time for you to get back on the road."

"It is," I said.

Her nose wrinkled as though she was about to sneeze and she put her hands in the pockets of her jeans, her shoulders shuddering against the early autumn chill. "We're having dinner," she said. "You want a burger?"

"I'm all right," I said. I looked past her at Gabe. He looked like some kind of ghost, caught between the yellowing lamplight and the sinking sun. He was chewing a bite and trying not to watch us, impossibly small against the coming night.

"You don't have Sancho to look after you," she said. "You'll need to be careful by yourself."

"I will," I said. "And I'll be back in a few months. I'm working a short season."

She didn't look like she believed me, and I guess I don't blame her. She just patted me once on my driving arm and withdrew her hand. But I meant it.

"We'll be here," is all she said, and I put the truck in gear and pulled away before I could say anything at all.

But I watched them out of my rearview mirror. I drove slow and watched her walk all the way back to Gabe.

The thing is, I can't barely see Gabe when I look at him. I hope it's okay that I tell you that. He looks like he might just flicker out of existence at any second, and I can't help but see you in his place. Looking at him, I know that the gap I'm walking between what I write to you and what I don't write, it's getting narrower every year.

I'm not going to sign your mother's paperwork, either. I called her and told her that not too long after we buried Junior. She's accepted it, and is moving ahead without me. I told her not to let me know how it turns out. I know what she needs, for your death to have an end, but I don't want anything to do with it.

She likes to think of grieving as a journey, your mother. A mappable line that begins with loss and ends with resolution. Or, as she put it, a hole that we're trying to fill with our conspiracy theories up here on the mesa. Something that we could heal if we just would. It's the same thing Dr. Court would like to believe, I'll bet. I'm pretty sure he's the only person happier about the lawsuit than her.

I know better. If I didn't before, I learned it from Junior. Nothing ends, ever. And nothing heals because there's nothing to heal. Losing you is my life now. There's no resolution to it. The main kick may fade some. Hell, it already has. Like I wrote this spring, returning to the mesa doesn't hurt like it did. But you're still there, everywhere. When

I sit on the porch, you're out there behind the Blanca Massif. When I sit in the cabin, you're what I can't see in the darkness through the window. You're in everything I see and don't see. Nobody gets to resolve that. We're all everything we've lost. Just as my fuckups as a father came, in part, from losses before you. Nothing ends, nothing heals.

Not that I'd have it any other way.

acknowledgments

I owe a huge debt of gratitude to all the folks who read *Cry Father* during the many stages of revision and were kind enough to say nice things. Their support was the only thing that kept me upright when everything about it seemed to be going wrong. They include Frank Bill, Ward Churchill, Christa Faust, Sophie Littlefield, Natsu Saito, and Charlie Stella.

Likewise, without the discernment and guidance of Gary Heidt, Oliver Gallmeister, and Adam Wilson, there's no doubt in my mind but that I'd still be wrestling with it, and with no end in sight. Nobody'd be reading it without them, that's for sure.

On the same lines, this book would have died in its infancy without my brother, Stephen Whitmer, who took a much-needed scouting expedition to the San Luis Valley with me, armed with nothing but Townes Van Zandt and a tent. It also couldn't have been written without David Staub, who, besides putting in countless hours talking about it on my back porch, took time out of his life to wander the Superfund sites and dive bars of North Denver. I also have to thank Joshua Mork, who, poor bastard, has probably heard me talk about it more than anybody. And I can't forget Kim and Robert Garcia, who I owe for the loan of their dog.

Which brings me to the one person who is, more than any other, responsible for this book: Lucas Bogan. Not only for all of the tree-trimming stories he let me steal, but for all the hiking, driving, story swapping, and daydreaming. In other words, for a lifetime of friendship. I owe you this one, man.

Lastly, I've been blessed with four parents and two children who I've done nothing to deserve. There's no excuse for how lucky I've been to have these six people in my life. I wake up thankful for them every day, which I hope they know.